JEANNIE WYCHERLEY

ISBN-13: 978-1726008884
ISBN-10: 1726008886

Sign up for Jeannie's newsletter: http://eepurl.com/cN3Q6L

Edited by Anna Bloom @ The Indie Hub
Cover design by JC Clarke of The Graphics Shed.

Given that it is rare for me to write anything my wonderful Mum would like to read, I am pleased that she will have a chance to enjoy this one.

No blood and guts in this one.

Carole Anne Sharp
Love you!

CONTENTS

CHAPTER ONE

We had chosen an early morning to say goodbye to Yasmin Daemonne. Now the mist rolled around the mourners, and without a lot of room in the small forest clearing, we huddled together by necessity. I glanced around at the congregation, amazed that my mother warranted such a gathering.

Yasmin and I had never really seen eye-to-eye.

Yet here were the great, the good ... and the not so good. Witches, wizards, warlocks and even the occasional Fae. Without exception everyone had dressed for the occasion. Clad in ceremonial mourning robes of black or midnight blue, some trimmed in ermine, the fairies in the finest silk. Witches from Yasmin's coven wore complex head-dresses of delicately woven twigs, dressed in moss and leaves and early blossoming spring flowers, freshly picked and prepared this morning no doubt, the whole shebang trimmed with black ribbon.

For my part, I had opted for plain black robes. They buttoned tightly at the neck, fitted snugly over my chest, rounded over my hips—thereby hiding a multitude of sins—and fell to the floor. Underneath these, I had chosen to wear a plain black wool dress and my thick-soled black boots. My robes rarely had an outing these days and as I'd put on weight in recent years, they were a tad snug for my liking. But what did it matter? I fully intended to burn the darn things when this ceremony had ended and my duties had been completed.

I hadn't been part of such a gathering since I finished school at eighteen, and that was over a decade ago, and I was finding the whole magickal ceremony overtly onerous.

The wizard in charge of the ceremony, the elder Luca Shadowmender, led us through a series of blessings, committing Yasmin to a world beyond, bidding her the fairest of walks in the Summerlands, where she would be at peace among her fore-mothers and fathers. We closed with a ritual of course; walking around the fire at the centre of the clearing, drawing on the elements, grounding ourselves in the earth but aspiring to soar through the air with Yasmin's spirit. I went through the motions with them, well versed in all aspects of witchcraft even though it was no longer my chosen path. Finally, Shadowmender called on the Goddess to lead Yasmin by the hand to a brighter day, and I took that as my cue to step forward and douse the flames of the fire with a handily placed pail of water.

Nothing magickal about that.

I remained in place, watching the smoke, with its varying shades of grey and white, as it coiled and uncoiled and drifted skywards. Perhaps the smoke was my mother's soul. Well, if it was, she was free now.

Shadowmender hobbled across the clearing to stand with me, leaning heavily on his staff and regarding me through rheumy eyes. I blinked back unexpected tears and offered him a half-smile.

"We're all very sorry for your loss, Alfhild," he murmured, directing nods at the others as they took their leave of the circle.

"Thank you," I replied. It seemed easier not to remind him that my mother and I had been estranged for several years. In any case, I was having some difficulty processing my feelings regarding Yasmin's death.

"She was a friend to all in need, a remarkable teacher and a powerful witch."

I acknowledged the tribute quietly. Maybe I had been the only person who had found her shrewish and difficult then? Or perhaps – more likely - the fault lay purely with me, her errant daughter. After all, I had rejected my calling as a witch so consistently and adamantly that my mother had despaired. I had pleaded with her to allow me to follow my own path, no matter where that would lead. In the heat of one particularly vicious argument she had scolded me, informed me of how ashamed she was, and banished me henceforth from her dwelling place.

Harsh words and recriminations. I shuddered at the memory of my mother spitting sparks of anger.

She had never understood that all I had ever wanted to be - was normal. To live among humans and do ordinary things. Whether that consisted of lounging in front of the television, or pogoing at a rock concert. I loved to bake – with flour and eggs and butter – rather than ground bat bones and gristlewhort foraged from a hedge. And yes, I chose to live in jeans and t-shirts rather than thick wool or velvet, or worse still, sturdily made clothes, all the better for outdoor activities. My one nod to my background? My goth make-up and penchant for black clothes. Yes, my jeans were black and my t-shirts were black and my eye-liner was black. But working as I tended to in pubs and night clubs, I never looked out of place.

Unfortunately, my mother had obstinately stuck to her guns and discounted any notion that her precious only daughter, Alfhild, could have a life outside the craft. Her total intransigence had eventually forced me to pack my bags and walk away for the sake of my sanity and my mother's blood pressure. That had been twelve years ago and we had rarely spoken since.

And now it was too late.

"I'm an orphan now," I intoned, so softly that Wizard Shadowmender could barely hear me.

The fire at my feet, supposedly doused with the water, gutted and sparked, and a single flame shot high into the air. I stared at it perplexed. What did it portend? In my mundane life it would simply mean I hadn't doused the flames well enough, but here in this clearing, surrounded by some of the most powerful witches and wizards in the land, I could only imagine that it must mean something else entirely.

The funeral supper was a jolly affair, held at The Full Moon, a public house in the centre of London on Celestial Street, known only to those who absolutely needed to know about it. Access to the pub was via an ordinary looking bookshop on Charing Cross Road. If you knew the right shelves to push - in the occult section naturally - you spun though to a dark, cobbled alley lined with all manner of useful magickal retail outlets, including: *Pointitatem's*, a wand shop obviously; *Basildon Bonded*, a stationer's – perfect for all your Book of Shadows requirements; *Fidl* - a supermarket specialising in frogs, toads, newts and all manner of sundries; and my personal favourite, *The Familiar Shoppe*, which sold an assortment of accessories for your familiars, whatever they might be, including cat scratching posts, cat toys, dog baskets, bird perches, and handmade decorative jewellery for unicorn horns.

The Full Moon was a tall, narrow pub, arranged over four floors, perfect for drinking and carousing, with rooms above where revellers could stay overnight. Today it was full to capacity, pulsing to the music emanating from the jukebox. Every day was Halloween at The Full Moon, and just now The Grateful Dead's *Sugar Magnolia* was blasting out of dozens of speakers, and entertaining the gathered throng. I wondered who had programmed the song, it being one of Yasmin's favourites.

I perched on a cushion strewn bench in the main bar, receiving consolations from each funeral guest in turn. I tried to be present in the moment, but increasingly found myself on automatic pilot, alternately commiserating or lamenting, smiling and chatting, as each situation—and each individual—warranted. My face hurt, my head ached, and beneath my robes I felt overly warm, the wool making me itch.

How much longer?

I glanced—surreptitiously I thought—at my watch, but when I looked up again found myself being appraised by a skinny woman with sharp features, her black robes tightly melded to her skeletal form and eyes that pierced my very soul.

Curiously, I stared back until, at last, the woman contrived a smile and slunk over to where I perched.

"Penelope Quigwell," she said and stuck out a bony hand. I took the woman's hand in my own plump and slightly sweaty palm, marvelling at the transparency of Penelope's skin. "I am your mother's lawyer."

"Was, surely?" I asked, a little acerbically. "You *were* my mother's lawyer. She's dead. That's what we're here for." I almost added the word, celebrating, but reined myself in. It probably wouldn't be appropriate, might be misunderstood, and I figured I'd been rude enough.

Penelope turned the corner of her mouth up. "I *am* your mother's lawyer until her estate has been disposed of."

"Estate?" I frowned. The dismal little hen coop where my mother dwelled, way down in the depths of the Somerset countryside didn't warrant so grand a title. A stray match would take care of it along with my mother's limited belongings. Yasmin had lived a simple life, with a hard wooden bench that doubled as both bed and sofa, a range with a large iron cauldron, and a larder where she saved her assortment of odds and ends for her peculiar collection of lotions and potions. She rarely kept any food in the house, and her clothes hung on a peg behind a curtain.

"Yes. Your late mother had a sizeable estate and you, my dear, are the sole heir."

"There must be some mistake," I shook my head. If Yasmin had money, why had she chosen to live so austerely?

Penelope drew herself upright, her face haughty. "No mistake." She handed over a card. "I'd like to see you in my office tomorrow, if you would be so kind. 10 a.m. sharp." With a snap of her head, Penelope spun on her spiky 6-inch heel, and disappeared into the throng of people gathered around the bar area.

I watched her make her way towards the exit, before glancing at the card in my hand. It was blank, but when I held it up, a cloud of black ink flooded across the stiff white vellum from top right to bottom left. It drifted across the card like dark sand, and then disappeared, leaving only a trace with the words:

Penelope Quigwell LLB
Lawyer
14b Celestial Street
London
W00 0OO

I sank back against the wood panelled wall behind me and stared around at the faces that claimed to have known and been friendly with my mother. I knew so few of them. For someone who had long eschewed the world of magic and witchcraft, I couldn't help but wish I knew more about what had been going on in my mother's life.

Chapter Two

I'd overslept.

This was a common enough occurrence given that my work pattern tended to be from 6 p.m. to 2 a.m. I rarely rose before midday, and disliked early mornings intensely. As far as I was concerned, sunrises were for losers.

Now I stretched in my single bed and glanced at the clock, acknowledging it was after 9, and vaguely remembering I had somewhere I needed to be.

Rats! My appointment with Penelope Quigwell.

I rolled out of bed, untangling myself from the covers. To shower or not to shower, that was the question. I lifted my arm and sniffed. No, I definitely needed to shower. Running a hand through my untamed mop of hair I realised I probably required a shampoo too. I stank of smoke and beer. Needing to get a move on, and praying my flatmate wasn't in the bathroom, I thundered down the hall like a fairy elephant and skidded to a stop in front of the steamy bathroom. I shared a house with three other women, and someone somewhere was always taking bath.

I was in luck.

Twenty minutes later, still damp from the shower, I hopped around my bedroom, scoping the floor for something smart enough to wear to a lawyer's office. My tiny bedroom was far too small to house a wardrobe, and the one built-in cupboard that existed overflowed with books and t-shirts. Running rapidly out of time, I plumped for a long black skirt, a plain black t-shirt and a black cardigan. Relatively smart.

In the hall, I glanced momentarily at my reflection, then smudged the remainder of yesterday's eye make-up a little and decided I'd do.

I'd have to, I'd run out of time.

Remarkably I landed myself a seat on the train.

I always enjoyed these short commuter journeys on the rickety old South London trains, casually observing my fellow travellers, while pretending to study the colourful maps and advertisements displayed above the top of their heads. Today I shared a carriage with the usual number of men and women in sharp suits and spotless shirts and blouses, no doubt scurrying between appointments and meetings; teenagers with huge headphones wrapped around their heads, nodding away to feral music; some Japanese tourists giggling into their phones and taking selfies; and a woman at the far end of the carriage who clutched a black velvet bag to her chest, rocking and muttering to herself, recognisably a witch, and down on her luck. As the train pulled into Charing Cross, I purposefully walked down the carriage and slipped a twenty pound note into the woman's hand. It wasn't much, but perhaps it would help her.

She crooned softly as I walked away, blessing me and wishing me good fortune. I returned her blessings and headed out of the station, glad to be in the open air on a spring day, even if it was smoggy and toxic in central London. I dashed along the road a little way to the Celestial Street Bookshop.

Celestial Street was quieter at this early time of day. Perhaps mornings aren't a good time for anyone of a darker persuasion? I hurriedly made my way into the alley, tuned left, slipping over the cobbles, searching for number 14. It transpired that number

14 was a clock shop called *Once Upon a Time.* I stood transfixed for a minute, staring through the window at the hundreds of clocks on display, all ticking and tocking and clicking and whirring, pendulums large and small swinging to and fro. As the large hand clicked over to the three, the shop erupted with a cacophony of chiming, beeping and chirruping. Dozens of cuckoos leapt out of their casings and shrieked open mouthed at me. I stifled a giggle. Working in there would be enough to drive you barmy.

The reminder of the time hurried me along.

Confused about exactly where I should be headed, I was about to enter the shop when I noticed a small black door to my left, with the characters 14b displayed in dull bronze.

I pushed a button for the intercom but nothing seemed to happen. With no noticeable bell to ring, and no knocker, I considered banging with my fist, but tried pushing the door first and found it on the latch. I made my way up a rickety flight of stairs onto the first landing, where a grumpy and sour-faced male receptionist, an older, thinner and more miserable version of Penelope Quigwell, wrote my name in a ledger. He made a great show of recording the time, before escorting me down a narrow hallway to the lawyer's office.

Penelope peered up from above her spectacles as I entered. Sitting behind an enormous and ornately carved wooden desk covered in green baize, she still managed to look intimidating in spite of her diminutive size.

"Ah, Ms Daemonne. At last. I was worried you weren't going to make it." I began to apologise but Penelope waved the words away. "Please take a seat," she requested.

I clip clopped across the shiny parquet floor to sit on the only other chair in the room. It was hard and uncomfortable, not somewhere you would want to remain for too long. I glanced around the room. The walls were lined with bookshelves, dozens of leather volumes neatly displayed on each shelf. Legal works. I wondered if Penelope had read all of them.

Penelope drew a file from a drawer under her desk and placed it carefully on the surface in front of her. The cover of the brief, once cream, had faded to a dull yellow. She opened it, turning over the first page, scanning the next one, and finally peering back towards me.

"Your mother's will was a simple one. You are

her only child and therefore her estate falls entirely to you."

I nodded, thinking again of the hen coop in the woods. "There really isn't very much to worry about though, is there?"

"Well that's not entirely true." Penelope steepled her fingers together and pursed her lips, regarding me with a certain amount of disdain. I cocked my head to one side and waited for Penelope to explain further.

"It is true that your mother had very little of her own, but in fact she was the beneficiary of your late father's will. Do you remember much about him?"

"Of course," I replied, a little irritably. Why wouldn't I? My father had been a benevolent wizard, fun and energetic. He loved to experiment with all manner of silly spells, and had made me howl with laughter at his escapades. I recalled fondly the yule lunch where he had caused the Brussel sprouts to explode when they arrived at the table. Yasmin had been far from amused but my father and I had chortled all afternoon. Memories such as this, reminded me of how much I missed him. He had disappeared when I was 12. My mother had been vague about what had happened, telling me only that he had died while on some kind of mission for his brotherhood. I had never found out much more about it.

"But I wasn't aware Dad had much that could be handed down either." I recalled the small stone cottage we had inhabited for some time, even after his death. "My mother sold our home when I was 18."

"Erik Daemonne was a wealthy man. He left his entire estate to your mother, on the understanding that she would pass it on to you when you were old enough. She elected never to draw on the income, and I have accounts for the past 18 years if you should wish to inspect the income over that period of time."

"Income? On what?"

"Your father left you an inn—"

"An inn? As in a pub?" I asked, unable to mask my amazement.

"Yes, with twelve guest rooms and owner's accommodation."

"Well, I'll be ..."

"Quite."

I blinked in shock. Of all the types of property I might have been left, surely an inn was right up my street. I'd been involved in the hospitality industry my entire adult life. Beer and ale, good food and music, those were the things I understood. How clever of my father to have left this for me. It was almost as if he'd foreseen what I would try and do with my life. But why hadn't I known about it? Why hadn't my mother said anything?

"The inn closed down three years ago, but until then it had been run by a manager. Obviously the staff had to be paid, and the inn had become run down. It wasn't profitable. It will need substantial investment."

My sense of euphoria evaporated. Basically I'd been left a dud, then? An expensive inheritance that I wouldn't be able to do anything with. Perhaps I should burn it down along with my mother's hen coop. Disappointment flooded through me. "I see."

"But the income from the cottages should help you fix it up, or I suppose you could sell the inn and live off the rental income."

"Cottages? Rental income?"

"Ah. I'm not really making myself clear, am I?" Penelope Quigwell smiled, or it may have been a grimace, I wasn't quite sure. "Your father owned a village—er ..." Penelope consulted the papers in front of her. "Whittlecombe in East Devon. The properties include a dozen tied cottages, a post office, a convenience store, a café and Whittle Inn itself. Oh and some adjoining land. Some pasture, a wood, that kind of thing."

"A wood?" What would I do with a wood?

Penelope consulted her papers again. "Yes, Speckled Wood it says here. Around ten acres." She scanned the paper. "Yes. There are perhaps two dozen or so other privately owned dwellings in and around the area that you won't derive any income from I'm afraid to say, but certainly, you shouldn't have any problems living within your means if you're sensible."

I felt my eyebrows disappear into my hairline. A dozen cottages? A post office? An inn? A wood? And a village? A *whole village*? What on earth was I going to do with a whole village?

Chapter Three

I hailed a taxi outside Honiton train station and loaded my bags into the back. I'd handed in my notice at the nightclub, kissed my lease on the tiny room in Lewisham goodbye, and bid a not-so-sorry farewell to London and everything the city had come to mean to me. This morning I had awoken with a renewed sense of purpose about life, and excitement skittered around my insides like mice in a cage.

That exhilaration had been forcibly muted by the laborious journey; apparently I'd boarded the slowest train known to witchkind. The train, fast to Reading, had then proceeded to stop at every single station possible. I hadn't been aware there were this many stations in the whole of England, let alone the West Country. Hadn't they all been closed in the nineteen sixties? Thank the Goddess I hadn't been travelling all the way down to Cornwall. Devon, it appeared, was quite far enough away from civilization as it was.

But now I'd arrived. And Devon was as beautiful as I remembered from my time holidaying by the coast as a child. I'd been vaguely aware that my father hailed from these parts, but given that we had settled further up country, towards London, in Somerset, I had never really considered my links to this incredibly beautiful county.

East Devon was a rolling patchwork quilt of green fields and forest. The land undulated up and down, down and up, coloured in a thousand—no, a hundred thousand—shades of green, before sloping inevitably and inexorably down to the sea.

And the roads? No romans had carved these. They were primordial paths that ancient man had picked out. Lanes meandered here and there, turning back on themselves and heading off at right angles. The signposts, those that I could spot as there didn't appear to be many in existence, seemed meaningless, pointing vaguely between two potential avenues of travel. Fortunately, the taxi driver seemed to know exactly where we were heading.

We arrived into Whittlecombe shortly after three thirty, and the driver pulled up outside a smart looking inn with soft red tiles on the roof, and hanging baskets on the veranda. I stared out in confusion. A freshly painted hanging sign proclaimed I'd arrived at The Hay Barn. I wound my window down to get a better look.

Across the road several locals were gathered outside the Post Office and convenience store, chatting away to each other. Down the road I could see a sandwich board placed on the grass verge outside a café. A row of thatched cottages slipped into the distance, each one painted a different pastel shade and prettier than the last.

"I don't think this is the right place." I leant forward to speak to the taxi driver.

"Oh beg your pardon, love," he replied cheerfully enough. "I thought you were after the inn at Whittlecombe?"

"The Whittle Inn," I said, and looked out again at the cheerful premises to my right, a sinking sensation in the pit of my stomach.

"Ah right you are then," he nodded his understanding and started the engine once more. We drove slowly away from The Hay Barn and I saw from the corner of my eye how those gathered outside the Post Office watched us curiously as we moved away.

We cruised past the cottages, looking dreamy in the afternoon sun. Close up I could see they needed fresh paint on the external walls, perhaps some attention to the doors and windows. The thatched roofs appeared to be in good repair which was a relief. I shuddered to think how much it would set me back to re-roof twelve cottages.

The dwellings petered out and the road became a single lane, curling away from the village and heading uphill. To one side were fields, and to the right, forest. A swift right turn—down the narrowest lane imaginable—took us through a tunnel of trees, the dappled sunlight making me blink as we moved speedily through shadow and back to sunshine. The road was pot holed, and although tarmacked, wild grass grew up through the middle. It was a road less travelled for sure.

The lane opened out into a clearing and I caught my first sight of Whittle Inn.

I had the door open and was leaping from the taxi almost before it had pulled to a stop. The driver ratcheted the handbrake as I stood beside the door and gazed in awe at the inn.

It must have been beautiful once. Who knew how old it was? Maybe fifteenth or sixteenth century? Perhaps older. Certainly it had been added to over the years. An Elizabethan veneer here, a Georgian building here, a Victorian extension there, and the adaptation of the stable block to create further accommodation at some time in the last century.

The first two storeys were black and white, appearing typically Elizabethan. The upper stories looked to me like something out of a Disney fairy tale, with turrets and arched windows. The first two floors of the building appeared to have buckled, listing dangerously to one side, but the upper floors pulled the whole building the other way.

Whittle Inn was wonky ... and I loved it at first sight.

Oh, to be sure it needed work. The paint was flaking from the walls, and peeling from the woodwork, and some of the plaster had fallen away, but even so, this was achievable. I couldn't see the roof from this low on the ground, but Penelope Quigwell had arranged for a surveyor to come and look at the inn in the morning, so I would find out more tomorrow about what needed doing and how much it would cost me.

The rumble of tyres on gravel behind me and a scattering of small stones alerted me to the fact that I had company. Of course. Penelope had arranged for the local estate agent to come out and hand over the keys to the inn and show me around. He pulled his silver Audi up next to us and hopped out of the car.

"Alfhild Daemonne?" he asked.

"Yes," I replied, trying to quell my exuberance.

"Jason Joplin from Hawke, Joplin and Harrow. I trust you had a pleasant journey and found Whittlecombe without any problems?"

"Thanks to my taxi driving friend here," I replied, shaking Jason's hand. "Let me just get my bags..."

"Please," Jason leaned back against his car as I rummaged in my handbag to find my purse. The taxi driver hauled my bags out of the boot and took them to the front door. I handed over what I owed him along with a hefty tip. I could afford that now. I was an heiress.

Pleased, the taxi-driver doffed an imaginary cap. "I hope you'll be very happy here," he said. "Although I suspect you might be better off staying in The Hay Loft for now."

I understood what he meant. Whittle Inn was dark. It hadn't been lived in for years. Who knew what horrors awaited me inside.

I didn't care.

I waved the taxi driver a cheery farewell and turned my attention back to Jason. He smiled greasily, and held out a ring of keys. The ring itself was rusted, and as big as a normal sized bangle. There must have been in excess of twenty keys hanging from the loop.

"Wow," I said, taken aback.

"Yes," Jason replied, obviously enjoying my surprise. "And that's just the inn. I have a box of keys back at the office that belong to the cottages and businesses that you own."

I shook my head. "Why would I need the keys for those? They belong to other people."

"They belong to you," Jason explained patiently. "You're a landlord now. For sure there are laws against you gaining access to those properties while they are leased, the tenants have rights after all. But, at the end of the day, you never know when you may have to go in, or send someone in, if your tenant doesn't pay their rents or stipends."

"Has that ever happened?" I asked. Penelope had told me that Hawke, Joplin and Harrow had been acting as agents to my father's estate for several decades, collecting rents and overseeing the drawing up of leases etc.

"Not to my knowledge," Jason replied. "Everyone loves Whittlecombe. No-one would want to run the risk of being evicted from the village."

That was a relief.

"Shall we go in?" Jason asked, and I nodded in excitement.

Inside, the inn was much as I had expected, shadowy and cold and unlived in. Once again, structurally everything appeared sound, although the décor was decidedly 1980s and not twenty-first century. We entered directly into the main bar, and I stood for a while taking in my new empire.

To my right a door led to a staircase that would take me up to the bedrooms. Dead ahead the wall was beige plasterboard, with a number of posters, yellowing with age, pinned to the wall. To my left was where all the action happened.

The serving bar itself was a beautiful slab of carved oak, darkened with age and countless layers of polish. Overhead were hooks for glasses, but where the optics would once have lived was nothing but beige wall, stained from splashes and spillages. The floor was covered in a heavy duty carpet and as I walked over it dust motes erupted into the air. They swirled merrily around in the muted sunbeams shining through the filthy windows.

Ugh.

Chairs and tables were piled up in one corner, looking like kindling for a bonfire. I poked around them. They seemed sturdy enough, although all of the styles and shapes were different.

To the right of the bar was a door that took me into a corridor, and brought me to two smaller rooms on the left, each with a stable style door, and a sign attached to the lower half. The first room was named 'The Snug' and the next room, 'The Nook'. Both had a fireplace, benches arranged in a u-shape and a large table. Good little meeting rooms that could be made cosy in no time.

Opposite these a staircase would take me up to my private quarters, but at the bottom of the stairs a door led through into a large old-fashioned kitchen with a range and several ovens, and boxes of utensils and pans in dull metal, as well as access to several large store rooms and the outside.

I pulled open a number of kitchen cupboards and found crockery galore. There was masses of it, much of the china appeared to be incredibly old, and again hardly any of it matched.

The more I poked around, the more I was falling in love with the place. The inn and its contents were ill fitting and mismatched, just like their new owner.

I was a wonky witch in a wonky inn and I had never felt more at home.

Upstairs I found more of the same. Quaint brass-framed beds with lumpy mattresses that stank of damp. Walls in desperate need of paint. Carpets that needed ripping up and discarding, and bathrooms with the most ancient plumbing imaginable. I had never clapped eyes on a toilet with an overhead cistern - outside of a museum at any rate - in my entire life.

The owner's quarters were small but cosy. A living room, a small personal kitchen, a bathroom and a larger bedroom, and an office that looked out over the woods beyond the back of the inn. Speckled Wood, I surmised. I could happily imagine myself ensconced at the large old desk in this room, staring out at the trees and watching the birds and squirrels live their own lives.

Smiling, I made my way to the window to gaze out over the grounds behind the inn. A garden that would likely catch the sun in the evening. I could place tables and benches out there and create a beer garden with lots of sparkling lights and wind chimes.

Perhaps I could install some water features and really turn the garden into a fairy paradise.

"You can see yourself living here, then?" Jason was asking, observing the spring in my step I was sure.

"Oh yes. It's going to need fixing up, but I can't wait to get started."

"Could take some time, I suppose."

"I have plenty of that," I responded merrily. "I'll put my back into it."

"Great. You'll have guests here before you know it."

He glanced up at the ceiling and made some notes on his tablet, probably about the staining up there. I'd need to get up in the loft and check out what was going on in the roof space. I would do that with the surveyor, I decided.

I turned for now to the windows and the view out the back. The windows were old, with lead diamond patterning, and an old fashioned clasp for the lock. I lifted a clasp up and pushed hard against the window. It eventually gave, albeit reluctantly, so that I could fling it wide and lean out.

To the right was the old stable block, more recently converted into another two bedrooms. I would need to inspect those too. It looked pretty rundown. Down below was a concrete yard area, presumably outside the back door. That would need prettifying.

A pile of rubbish had been left in the middle of the patio area, little more than a large bundle of rags by the look of it.

Wasn't it?

Something amongst the pile of rags glinted, catching the sunlight, and I felt a sudden twang in the pit of my stomach.

There was something odd about the pile, something that caused my sixth sense to sit up and take notice. "What's that, down there?" I asked Jason and he came up behind me to peer out. I moved out of his way so that he could get a better look.

"Rubbish maybe?" he said, but I could hear the doubt in his voice.

I shook my head, certain that it wasn't. "I'm going to have a closer look," I said and hurried out of my new quarters and back down the stairs. The back door was heavy and bowed, with numerous locks and bolts. I surveyed the heavy bolts while waiting for Jason to catch up with me. He sorted through the keys, looking for the right one, drawing a blank again and again.

"Open it," I urged.

"It must be here somewhere," he said, tutting in frustration. When he got to the end of the ring he started again. And then again. It took an age. The third time around, just as I was beginning to lose hope, the very first key fit the lock like a glove. He turned it and I heard the tumblers fall.

Jason drew back the dead bolts top and bottom, as I hopped impatiently beside him. Finally, the door was flung open and he stood back to let me through first. I burst out into the late afternoon sunshine and stalked eight or nine paces to where the pile of rags lay on what passed for a patio.

Timidly, I bent down and yanked on one piece of black cloth. It was caught, wrapped around something heavy. As I tugged harder the bundle unrolled, and a gnarled hand, as pale as the underbelly of a shark, flopped onto the concrete slab beside my foot. On one of the milky-grey fingers, a ruby ring, speckled with gold, glittered up at me in the sunshine.

Startled, I shot backwards, colliding with the estate agent hovering behind me.

"Jason?" I said. "I think I may just have received my first guest."

CHAPTER FOUR

I spent the night, albeit a shortened one, at The Hay Barn after all. By the time the paramedics had finished with the body and taken it away, and the police had completed their questioning of Jason and myself, it had become apparent that staying at the inn alone was not such a great idea. Jason kindly drove me back into the village and I checked in just before eleven. I threw myself on the bed in my anonymous room, loneliness and depression washing through me.

Finding the body on my new back doorstep had shaken me to my core. I'd opted not to disturb it any more than I already had, it being apparent to me that no-one sporting that particular skin tone could possibly still be alive. Over and over I replayed the moment the hand had flopped into view at my feet, and lamented the fact that The Hay Barn had neither a bar in the room, nor a 24-hour bar downstairs. Instead, I soothed myself by nursing a cup of overly strong tea made in the tiniest cup in the world, with the smallest possible pod of long life milk, before showering and trying to settle myself enough to sleep.

Alas, sleep eluded me for the most part. I lay on the comfortable bed, in the immaculate room with my eyes wide open, comparing Whittle Inn to The Hay Barn, somewhat unfavourably. The Hay Barn was everything that I would have intended for Whittle Inn. The furnishings were hardy, plain and comfortable, the décor contemporary. The food on offer was the usual fare of lamb shanks, gammon and egg, and steak and chips. The Hay Barn offered everything a visitor to the area would want or need.

I was worried. Did the existence of The Hay Barn necessarily mean there wasn't enough room in the village for another inn? That would be the case if I attempted to offer something very similar, surely? Where did that leave me with my own plans? How could I make Whittle Inn different?

I tossed and turned and then when the dawn made itself known, I listened to a cacophony of birdsong. For some odd reason, the rambunctious twittering was enough to finally send me into a deep sleep.

I awoke, feeling groggy and headachey a little after nine. I considered rolling over and sleeping some more, certainly at home in Lewisham I would have done, but that thought brought me to my senses. I no longer had a home in Lewisham. I had a new life here in Whittlecombe and I was required to check out of The Hay Barn by 11 am. Breakfast was waiting for me downstairs, and I needed to meet the police back at Whittle Inn at midday.

Breakfast was served directly to me in the dining room. I noted with glee the greasy smudges on the table, and the salt grains that had worked their way under the laminated surface. The Hay Barn, far from perfect after all, required a deep clean.

Feeling smug, I opted for an English breakfast, the full works – including a juicy sausage, hash browns, and mushrooms. It looked good but tasted bland, the bacon being too thinly sliced. And the plates weren't china, instead mass produced from a well-known Swedish superstore. I tucked in anyway, and mopped up the juices with an extra slice of toast. I was supposed to be watching my weight, but I had a feeling the extra calories might come in useful today, and I needed some comforting.

I wiped my fingers clean on the paper serviette with some distaste as the waitress descended on my table with a teapot in one hand and a coffee pot in the other. She was a short young woman, aged around twenty or so, with hair dyed bright red and piercings in her eyebrow and nose. "Would you like any more coffee or tea?" she asked and I opted for coffee. I needed the lift.

"Thank you," I said, wondering whether to ask for more toast.

"You're welcome. Do you have any plans for today?" she asked cheerily. I looked up into her open face. She seemed genuinely interested. I checked out her name badge. Charity.

"I kind of do," I said. "I'm the new owner of Whittle Inn. I've plenty to be getting on with."

"Really?" exclaimed Charity with great excitement. "Then you'll know all about the murder! The whole village is buzzing with the news this morning."

"Murder?" I said, wondering whether the police had confirmed this. I guess you didn't need to be a detective to figure out that it probably was, assuming that the body had been killed elsewhere, wrapped in material and dumped. I wasn't quite so sure this scenario was the only possibility, but I would bow to the police's superior knowledge.

"That's what they're saying."

I frowned, wondering who 'they' were.

Charity noticed the look on my face and grimaced. "Sorry. It's not very nice for you, is it? Will you be staying with us for a while? How long before you're intending to move into the old inn?"

"Today with any luck," I replied. "If the police release it back to me, and if I can get the water switched on. Which reminds me, I need to make some phone calls." I fished around in my bag for my mobile.

Charity smiled. "Well if you need anything, give me a shout. I guess you're my new landlord too. I live in Snow Cottage," she said, as if that meant anything to me, but I guessed it was the name of one of the cottages belonging to the estate.

"Thank you, Charity. That's really lovely of you." I waited for her to walk away and started thumbing through my contacts for the numbers I needed.

When a shadow fell over my table for a second time, I assumed that Charity had returned, but this time it was an older gentleman, with a shock of neatly cut white hair, wearing an expensive tweed jacket and baggy corduroy trousers. I didn't recognise him.

"Did I hear you say you're the new owner of Whittle Inn?" he asked shortly, his plummy accent pointing to an over-privileged background of public school and Oxbridge. He put my teeth on edge straight away.

"Yes," I said, refraining from adding 'you did hear that if you were eavesdropping on a private conversation.' I didn't offer any further explanation. He waited a moment and then when I wouldn't play ball with him, he sniffed. A contemptuous sound if ever I heard one.

"It's in a fair state of decay, the old inn, isn't it?"

"It seems structurally sound to me," I replied smoothly. "Nothing that can't be taken care of, I'm sure."

"Have you thought about bulldozing it?"

"No." The cheek of the man.

"I mean to say," he carried on blustering as though I hadn't already replied to him, "have you seen the list on that building?"

"I should think the inn's been wonky since the day it was built," I said and smiled. "Rather like the leaning tower of Pisa. Historically lopsided."

He harrumphed. "You should talk to my lawyer.

I'll give you a good price for the inn and the land it's standing on."

"Should I?" I asked, politely enough, but inside I was beginning to bristle. "And who exactly are you?"

"Gladstone Talbot-Lloyd." He held out his hand and at first I thought he wanted to shake mine, but as I put mine out in automatic response I saw that he was actually offering me a business card. "This is my lawyer's card. He'll deal with everything."

Dumbfounded, I took the card and looked up at him. "I can assure you, Mr Talbot-Lloyd, I won't be putting the inn up for sale. I fully intend to open it up again and make a success of it."

"Then you're a fool," he sneered. "You should have stayed in London. A young woman like you can succeed—in some small measure at least—up there in the big city. Down here, we don't take kindly to jumped up entrepreneurs and the like."

"I'm no jumped up entrepreneur," I seethed. "I have years of experience in hospitality. I'll be working hard to make my business a success."

"It won't be enough. Take my word for it," Talbot-Lloyd sneered. As if I would take anything he said and give him a penny for it. "You need a name. You need to *be* someone. You need family behind you. My understanding is you have no-one."

His words stung, but the truth at the core of them pulled me up sharply. Perhaps he was right and I wouldn't be able to achieve what I'd set my heart on. He'd said I needed a family behind me. What family could I draw upon? I had no-one. They were all dead.

But now as I considered them – my father and his family, all the generations who had lived in the inn before me – I found my anxiety dissipated. My mind cleared and my fury ebbed away. This man had no idea who or what he was dealing with. Clearly.

"Do you believe in ghosts, Mr Talbot-Lloyd?" I asked innocently.

"What?" he puffed his chest out, "What are you talking about? Of course I don't believe in ghosts."

"Well perhaps you should do." I stood up, straightened my spine and looked him straight in the eye. Generations of my father's family must surely have been haunting the corridors of Whittle Inn for centuries. No doubt they walked there still and would be keeping me good company. "My family are totally behind me, in spirit if nothing else."

I walked away. At the exit to the dining room I turned back and harrumphed back at him. "The inn is not for sale, Mr Talbot-Lloyd. Good day to you."

Chapter Five

Forty minutes later I remembered why London had held such an allure for me as a seventeen-year-old, whilst my Somerset home had not. The nearest taxi firm operating around Whittlecombe was located miles away, the bus service was negligible, and it looked like it would be faster for me to walk to Whittle Inn than wait for a ride.

I set out at a brisk pace, happy that I hadn't brought much into the village with me the previous evening. I'd left all my bags behind at the insistence of the police who hadn't wanted me to disturb their scene any more than I already had done.

The day was fine, the sky blue and the sun climbing high, and a walk would be far from unpleasant. I observed the shop and post office from across the road, and decided to pop in and collect some necessities. With any luck the power and water would be restored to the inn before the end of the day, and it would be great to make tea and a sandwich in my own kitchen.

The door stood ajar so I walked straight in. Time had obviously stood still here in Whittlecombe. The old fashioned counter, and the shelving behind it, reminded me of pictures in history books. One wall displayed colourful jars of sweets, and another tins and packets of food. The third wall was covered in soap powder, washing up liquid and other household necessities. I'd get all my necessities, right here, right now, but if I wanted lemongrass and mushroom ketchup, I'd probably have to order online or take a trip to a larger supermarket in the nearest town.

I hovered by the newspapers. The local rag had got hold of the 'murder at the inn' story and now Whittle Inn was plastered over the front page for all the wrong reasons. I cringed.

"Good morning, madam," chimed a perky voice behind the counter. I turned to observe a plump lady wearing a cream pinny smiling at me. "Can I be of assistance?" she asked.

"Hello, good morning, and yes," I said and her beam broadened. "I need a few things ... erm ... tea, milk, butter, sugar, cheese, bread."

"That sounds like the making of a grand picnic," the woman said. "Are you on holiday? Staying somewhere close?"

I had to come clean. The shop was another property leased from the estate. Sooner or later she would have to know who I was. I hoped she wouldn't hate me but I'd never had a great relationship with any of the landlords I'd rented property from. How could you not see them as money-grabbers?

"My name is Alfhild Daemonne. I'm the new owner of Whittle Inn and I've inherited all my father's properties." I flushed slightly, and ducked my head so the woman couldn't see my embarrassment.

She studied me seriously for a moment, looking me up and down. Then she shook her head in disbelief and broke out into another wide smile. "Well, fancy that!" She skipped out from behind the counter. "It's lovely to meet you. I'm Rhona Marsh and I run the shop here with my husband, Stanley. We knew there was a new owner, but imagined we wouldn't get to meet them."

"Why's that?" I asked as she pumped my hand up and down.

"Well ... you'll find there's many absentee landlords in these parts nowadays. They buy up the property and let it out, and their agents do all the work and organise the maintenance. It's impersonal, I feel." She scrutinised my face. "I hope I'm not speaking out of turn, Ms Daemonne."

"Oh call me Alf, please."

"Alf. Such a laddish name for a beautiful woman!"

I laughed, liking Rhona more and more. Her openness and honesty and gentle flattery was a breath of fresh air. There were no sides to her. She began to gather together the things I'd asked for.

"So what are your plans?" she asked curiously. "Will you stick around?"

I nodded and looked through the window, across the road to The Hay Barn. "Yes. I had planned to restore the inn, now I'm not so sure what I'll do with it."

She followed my gaze. "Too much competition, you think?"

"Yes."

"Mm," she pursed her lips thoughtfully. "It's all about how you find your market isn't it?" She gestured around at the shelves. "It's about knowing what to sell and to whom. Once you have that nailed you're home and dry."

"Sage advice," I said, unsure how to attract a different clientele to such a small village. I glanced at the newspaper headline again. "I suppose I'd better get back. The police will be waiting for me."

"That's a terrible introduction to your new home," said Rhona. "Such a shock for you. Who was he? Do you know?"

"I know very little," I said and picked up a copy of the newspaper to add to my pile of goodies. Perhaps I could find out something new by reading the story. "It's so sad though."

"It is. Whittlecombe is generally such a sleepy little village. You must wonder what you've let yourself in for." Rhona laughed merrily. "Won't you be worried, being up at the inn on your own?"

I thought about my encounter with Talbot-Lloyd and remembered the vision I'd had of my father's family.

"I think I'll be fine."

"How are you getting back? I didn't see a car."

"Looks like I'm walking," I said, eyeing the weight of the bag she was about to hand over to me with dismay.

"Nonsense," Rhona replied. "We can't have that. A valuable new customer like yourself. I'll get Stan to run you." Before I could protest she had stuck her head behind the door and was calling for her husband. "It's not a problem," she said, cutting me off. "Now is there anything else you'd like, given that you won't have to carry it by yourself anymore, or shall I ring this up for you?"

Chapter Six

I found Detective Gilchrist leaning against his car waiting for me. My new friend Stanley unloaded the boxes of supplies I'd asked for—I'd figured I might as well take advantage of the lift back to the inn and buy up half the little shop's cleaning materials—while I presented myself to the officer, a little tardily to be fair. The story of my life.

"Good afternoon, Ms Daemonne," he said and arched an eyebrow. He was a good looking man, late thirties, tall and blonde, Scandinavian looking you might say, heavy set and slightly grizzled.

"Have you been standing there all night, Detective?" I smiled, hoping he would forgive me for my late arrival.

"It certainly feels like it." Gilchrist rubbed a huge paw over his eyes and face. I had a sudden yearning to reach out and stroke the stubble there myself. That would never do.

"I have the makings for tea and coffee," I announced excitedly, gesturing at the boxes Stanley was busy unloading. "If I have electricity too, I could make you a drink."

"That would be great," Gilchrist said and I turned for the front door.

"Oh," I said, pulling myself up short. "Am I allowed back in?"

"Yes, forensics are finished. They found nothing in the inn of any use, no disturbance or forced entry so you're free to get on. They'll need access out the back for the rest of the day probably, so I would avoid using the back door or garden, if you don't mind?"

"No, of course not. That's fine," I said and with some relief pushed open the main door to the inn.

"Where would you like these?" Stanley called from behind me.

"Just in here, please," I instructed, flicking switches on the wall. To my delight, the lights blinked on. "We have electricity," I crowed. Yes, it did feel like a triumph. What I found less delightful was the way in which the sudden illumination highlighted how much of a mess the bar was in, and in all its technicolour detail.

My bags remained where I'd dumped them the previous day. I fished out the small kettle I'd brought with me and quickly searched through the boxes Stanley was fetching, in order to locate the coffee, milk and a bottle of water. I intended to let the water run through the system for a while before I trusted it to be properly drinkable.

"I have these plastic mugs if that's okay? Sorry they're not very fancy," I said, holding up one pink beaker and one purple one. "I wasn't sure what I'd find here, or how usable anything would be, so I brought what I thought would be essential."

Gilchrist smiled, "Very enterprising of you. I don't care how it comes so long as it's wet and it keeps me awake."

"I'll make sure it's strong then."

Stanley brought in the last of the boxes. "That's all for now," he announced.

"Thanks so much," I said. "I really appreciate it."

"No problem, my love. Let us know if you need anything else. We're always happy to deliver around the village."

"Would you like a coffee?" I asked brandishing my jar of instant.

"No, I'd best be getting back. I'm sure Rhona will have a list of other jobs I have to complete before lunch," he winked at me, and I waved him away with relief. I only had two beakers, and given that I fancied another hit of caffeine myself, I didn't want to give mine up.

I handed Gilchrist his drink and we pulled out a couple of chairs from the pile to sit on.

"What news do you have for me?" I asked. "I understand it was a man, and that's about all I know."

"It was a man," Gilchrist confirmed. "An older chap. We think in his late sixties, early seventies. He had no ID on him, so at this stage we have no idea who he is or where he came from. There had been no attempt at a forcible entry. The property was secure, no forced doors or windows, nothing broken, and as far as it is possible to tell, there doesn't appear to be anything here that shouldn't be. Have you noticed anything missing?"

I shook my head. "To be honest, yesterday was the first time I've set foot in the property so I'm probably not the best person to ask. But then again, I'm not sure who'd know. My mother's lawyer has never been here, and I had the impression that although Hawke, Joplin and Harrow have been managing the estate, it's all a bit hands off really."

Gilchrist nodded. "Yes, I thought as much."

"So you have no leads on who the man is at all?"

"Not at this time but we'll put out a nationwide alert and see what we can discover. There is a database of missing persons, so we'll check for matches of anyone on there, and maybe put out an appeal for information with an artist's impression."

"Okay," I said, feeling sad for the old fella.

"I'd like to show you the likeness once our artist has had a chance to create if, if that's alright with you."

"Of course. Anything to be of assistance, although I don't know anybody from around here at all."

"Well, he may have been visiting. And of course, one of the angles I'll need to look at was whether he was connected to the inn in some way."

"Yes." That made sense. "What was the cause of death?"

"Undetermined at the moment. Nothing obvious. The pathologist will be having a closer look this afternoon."

"I see," I shuddered. The dead didn't bother me much, as a witch I naturally accepted the notion that the body is merely a husk. Death is a release and the start of something new. However, I didn't want to dwell on what happened to the body once it was removed from the murder scene.

"For now, all that remains for me to do is to suggest you take your own safety very seriously, Ms Daemonne. Are you intending on staying here alone?"

"At the inn? Yes, it's my home now. There is no-one else to stay with me." I shrugged. "But don't worry. I can take care of myself."

"I'm guessing there's no landline installed here yet, but I assume you have a mobile?" Gilchrist fished around in the pocket of his jacket for his card. "This is me. You can call whenever you like. But if it's an emergency you dial 999, alright?"

"No problem," I said. "And I do have a mobile of course."

"Good. Text me so I can add your number." He stood. "Right. I'd better head back to the station and see how we're doing with identifying this guy."

I escorted Gilchrist to the door and accepted his beaker when he returned it to me.

"Thanks for the coffee," he said.

"I hope it was strong enough."

"It tarred my insides, so I'd say it sufficed." He winked. "Stay safe now, and don't forget to text me your number."

"I won't. I promise."

I followed him out and watched him drive away, then turned back to look at the inn.

My inn.

Nothing about it felt threatening. In fact, I almost imagined as I walked back inside that it sighed contentedly.

"I'm here to love you," I said. "I'm going to restore you to your former glory and between us we are going to carve out this new life and make it work."

With my hands on my hips I gazed around.

"But where on earth do I start?"

Six hours later, with hair like straw, I collapsed on the front step swigging from a bottle of water and wiping dust out of my eyes, trying to shift the thick ball of grit lodged in my throat. Oh to be a cat, I lamented, so I could cough up whatever was causing offence. Exhausted, I leaned against the door jamb, pondering the job ahead of me.

I recognised I needed at least one habitable space as soon as possible. Somewhere I could live, work and organise myself. A centre for operations so to speak. It therefore made sense, to start on my own quarters and make a few rooms at least vaguely habitable.

With the water on and the electricity restored, I could start cleaning, but I wanted a completely clean slate and that meant ripping up the carpets, peeling off wallpaper and removing partition walls.

I'd started with carpets. A great idea in theory, but oh! It had quickly turned into the most horrendous job. The floorcoverings were ancient. They must have been laid in the year dot. They were ingrained with dust and filth and who knows what else. It took all of my strength to tug them loose, starting in one corner and then hauling with all my might to unstick them from the floor. I'm not a slight woman, in fact there's plenty of bulk about me, but gee, I was going to need an army of helpers if I wanted to make any headway.

That was as far as I managed to get before the surveyor turned up. A tall man in a grey suit and sporting a hard hat, he arrived in an expensive Volvo, driving too quickly for the conditions, bouncing the car over the potholes, and almost spinning out as he braked hard on the loose gravel of the drive.

"It's the very devil to find this place," he

complained when I came out to greet him. "I'm looking for Mrs Daemonne?"

"Ms Daemonne?" I queried. "Will I do? I'm afraid my mother is recently deceased."

He looked me up and down with some distaste, echoes of my encounter with Gladstone Talbot-Lloyd sprang to mind.

"I see," he said, although clearly he wished I was someone older, wiser and perhaps more experienced in the ways of inn surveying. I was going to fail him on so many levels.

"Charles Pimm," he said and offered his hand for a limp-wristed handshake. I shook it with my own grime covered sweaty paw, and hid my smirk of amusement at his evident revulsion.

There followed a dull two hours where I traipsed around after him as he shone his torch into dusty corners and ummed and ahhed with annoying regularity. I peered over his shoulder, noting the cobwebs and dead rodents in inaccessible places. We gingerly climbed the ricketiest of staircases up to the loft and I was relieved to discover that the attic was properly boarded and floored. Best of all, there was no sign of damp. The roof lining appeared to be intact and that had been my main worry.

Less heartening was the amount of rubbish:

boxes, steamer trunks, furniture, bedsteads, mattresses, hat boxes and suitcases were generously littered throughout the space. I don't think I'd ever seen so much tat in one place. I stared aghast – wondering what on earth I would do with it all. I gingerly opened one suitcase to discover among the layers of old tissue paper, beautifully beaded and embroidered clothes, probably from the 1920s. It was a treasure trove to be sure, but the thought of sorting through it all didn't fill me with delight.

Against one of the joints, I spotted a number of paintings, standing back to back and partially covered by a sheet. I leant over them and pulled the sheet back, exposing the top one, a portrait of a rather forbidding looking woman in an evening dress and tiara. Beneath her, a gentleman with a white beard. I flipped through the heavy canvases, examining each image, and wondering who they were until an impatient tut behind me interrupted my reverie.

"I'd like to look out the back now, if I may."

Startled, I turned too quickly and smacked my head on a beam. "Out the back?" I repeated stupidly, rubbing my crown.

"Outside? The back of the inn?" He could barely hold back the contempt in his voice.

"Ah, right. That'll be a no then," I said.

"Because?" he asked, raising his eyebrows in disapproval.

"Because it's a murder scene." I explained patiently. "I found a body out the back, not even twenty-four hours ago. The police have asked me not to go out there for now, as their forensic team are still working there." Well I assumed they were, I hadn't taken much notice to be honest. I'd been far too busy listening to this man grunt non-committedly as I plodded after him all afternoon.

"I see." He made a series of clicking noises with his tongue against his teeth. I had to hold myself in check, to prevent my growing urge to throttle him. "Very well then. In that case I think we're finished here. I'll write up my report and let you have a copy."

"Can you share the headlines?" I asked and he blinked at me in confusion. "I mean, just tell me if the building is going to fall down any time soon?" I clarified.

"It will all be in my report," he said, his tone smug.

"Fine," I said, rolling my eyes with complete exasperation. Closing the attic door on the chaos within, I gestured for him to head down the stairs ahead of me.

I saw him out and opened a bottle of water,

draining a litre in seconds flat, then made my way back upstairs to open the taps and run water into my bathtub as the first step in ensuring the inn's pipes were clean.

Now I could think about stripping the walls in earnest.

It had been a long day on very little sleep and to say I felt daunted by the task in hand was an understatement. The more I stripped the walls, and pulled up carpets, the more apparent it became just how big an undertaking this was going to be. Dragging the carpets downstairs to throw out the front reminded me that I needed to hire in a skip. Possibly I needed to hire in a fleet of skips.

By 6 p.m. I was exhausted and kicking myself for not purchasing a bottle of wine at the shop along with all the cleaning products. It would require an impressive amount of Alf fuel to undertake a job this big. Wine, chocolate, coffee and cake were top of my list.

Sitting on my front step, I could feel the weariness sinking into my bones. I suddenly found myself longing for the tiny room in my house share in

Lewisham. Just the familiarity of it. The cosiness. It had never been beautifully clean and tidy, far from it, but I'd never had to worry about it or take responsibility for it either. Now here I was, the landlord of numerous properties I hadn't even inspected, with the mammoth task of putting the inn to work. I couldn't help but wonder whether I'd bitten off more than I could chew.

Sighing, I was about to stand and head back inside for some more punishment, when a woman with a large hairy lurcher came up the drive. In her late fifties I would say, she was an odd sight, dressed in green Wellington boots, a shapeless knee length summer dress covered in small colourful flowers, a home knitted cardigan in an odd shade of mustard green that clashed with the wellies, and a large brown rain hat. Her outfit covered all weather eventualities.

"Hello!" she hailed me, as jolly as she looked, she sounded well-to-do. Possibly not quite of Gladstone Talbot-Lloyd's class, but certainly only one step down on the ladder of poshness.

"Hello," I said and smiled at the dog as he came over to sniff me and find out what I was all about.

"Hope you don't mind Jasper, here?"

"He's a curious fellow," I said as he proceeded to sniff me all over.

"As all dogs are if they're doing their jobs correctly."

"Does Jasper have a job?" I asked, wondering whether she was one of the hunting fraternity, loved and loathed in equal measures in the English countryside.

"No, he doesn't work in that sense. He's just my companion." She made a clicking noise to call him to heel, and he pattered obediently to her side, looking up, perhaps waiting for a treat. She relented and chucked him under the chin and allowed him to wander off once more. He sniffed around the front of the inn. "He'd probably make a good poacher's dog though."

"Are there many of those around here?" I asked.

"Oh yes," the woman trilled cheerfully. "Are you planning on keeping hens or livestock at all?"

Her question made me think of my mother. "No, I shouldn't have thought so." This woman already knew I was the owner of the inn then. She had the advantage over me. "I'm Alf Daemonne."

She stuck out her hand to give me a warm and strong handshake. "Millicent Ballicott. I knew your father."

"You did?" I couldn't hide my astonishment at this news. No one had ever uttered those magic words to me before.

"Yes, when we were young children. We played together. He grew into a lovely man. Very generous." She scrutinized me through pale blue eyes. "You have a look of him about you."

"Really?"

"Yes. You have his colouring and chin. You must have your mother's eyes though." Millicent looked at me intently for a few moments longer as though trying to read my mind. I could see a question half-formed on her face. She evidently knew about my family's odd heritage.

"You don't use the craft," she said finally.

"No," I responded, and for the first time in many years I saw myself the way others of my kind might. Millicent was disappointed. She peered at me, down her nose, the same way my mother and her friends had always done, with a slight furrowing of the brow.

"Why?" she asked, and although she kept her tone light, the weight of the subject hung heavily between us.

I shrugged. "It isn't for me. I have no need of it."

Millicent looked knowingly at me and smiled.

"You mean you haven't had need of it, yet." She emphasised the last word.

I didn't reply, reluctant as ever to discuss my reasons for not choosing to use my skills as a witch. Instead I allowed my attention to drift back to Jasper.

"Better not let him go around the back," I said. He appeared to be heading that way, following a scent he'd picked out.

"Ah yes. Your murder," Millicent said and whistled for Jasper to return. He came back happily enough and headed for the trees leading back down the lane, intent on sniffing for squirrels.

"Yes."

"Any word on who the victim was?"

"No, not yet. Nor how he died."

"You found the body I heard?" I nodded. "Did you not have any inkling at all?"

Puzzled, I shook my head. What did she mean? "Of how he died? No. Why would I? I'm not a doctor."

"Well …" she began to answer but hesitated. "Never mind." She checked on Jasper, then turned back to me. "You're intent on making a go of the inn?"

"If I can." I could hear the lack of excitement in

my own voice. “I wanted to. Was determined to even, but now ...”

“Now?” Millicent asked, her expression kind.

“Maybe I’ll never be able to find people who’d want stay here. What with the murder and all. And the inn is old. Plus ... The Hay Loft is so close. Perhaps I’d be wiser just to sell the inn and land and move on with my life.”

“Sell it to Gladstone Talbot-Lloyd?”

“He seems to want it. How did you know that?”

“It’s no secret. He’s been after this old place for years. Since your father inherited it, and maybe even before that.”

“I wasn’t aware of that.”

“Everyone in the village knows about his lust for this land. He’s a foul man, that Talbot-Lloyd. Don’t let him bully you into doing anything you don’t want to.”

“But the murder? Maybe it’s a bad omen?”

Millicent clucked and looked annoyed. “Alfhild. You’re named after your father’s grandmother. She was a spectacular witch, but I don’t see much of her backbone in you. Maybe the murder is a bad omen. But equally, maybe you’re supposed to think that way.”

I pondered on what she was saying. "You think someone is out to get me?"

"It's probably nothing personal. But look at you." She gestured at me. "You're so young, and you're a woman on your own. In some people's eyes that makes you an easy target. A little bit of pressure and you'll take off, back to where you came from, with your tail between your legs."

I started to protest, but of course, not ten minutes before that was exactly what I was considering doing.

"Selling the land would be an easy and somewhat attractive proposition for you, I'm sure. Retire on the proceeds. Live like a queen. You'd never have to worry about money again." Millicent stepped closer, her eyes twinkling at me. "But if you're anything like your grandmother, I'm guessing that an easy life is not for you. Sure you'll want adventures, but by the same token you want a life that challenges you. This inn is that challenge. You'll have to be canny. But you can do it. Ready it for the right clientele."

Her words were a salve on my soul. Something heavy, that had been weighing me down all day, seemed to lift from my shoulders. Her words chimed with what Rhona had said about finding the right customers. Not that I had any idea who they might be yet.

"But, there's so much to do," I said. My token and final protest.

"You need help. I know just the person. I'll send him along tomorrow."

CHAPTER SEVEN

Once Millicent had strolled off in the direction of the village with Jasper in tow, I decided to go for a walk myself. It was time to familiarise myself with Speckled Wood, lying at the edge of the grounds behind the inn. I was probably dehydrated and I was certainly tired. The clean air would soothe my aching head and with any luck help me sleep.

Birds twittered in the trees as I skirted the police cordon, *Police – Do Not Cross*, emblazoned in blue on white tape. There had been no activity here since this morning, and there were no signs of an ongoing investigation. With any luck the police would release the yard and the kitchen back to me in the morning.

I nodded at the space where the body had been, in tribute to a life lost. Perhaps he had been a passing itinerant, or maybe he had been hanging out in the woods. Whatever, it was a sad start to my tenure.

As I'd hoped, the forest air was clean and clear, the air vibrating with life itself and lifting my solemn mood. The trees sang to me as I walked among them. You don't need to be a witch, even one as reluctant as I, to appreciate nature, but it certainly helps. Every bud, every leaf, every fern, every beetle—they called to me as I walked among them. I basked in the energy of the wood, breathed deeply and reinvigorated each cell within my body, stretching my spine and my tired muscles until I felt refreshed and calm once more. I stopped occasionally to gaze in wonder at a section of bark, or a clump of roots. I dragged my fingers over ridges, or pulled branches close to my nose to inhale the fresh scent of Mother Earth and all her bounty.

Entering a small clearing at the centre of the wood, I found a number of benches arranged in a circle. I plonked myself down on one to rest for a moment, noticing that the shadows had grown longer. It was time to turn back. I was intent on heading back to the inn and a feast of cheese and tomato sandwiches, when something odd caught my eye. A burn mark on the ground, where the scrub had been scorched. I poked about with my foot. The scar on the ground had been carefully disguised by twigs and branches and a scattering of organic mulch, but if you looked carefully you could see that the camouflage was an artifice. The ground had been swept clean but something had scorched the earth here, and then the evidence had been covered over.

I swivelled on the spot peering beyond the trees, and through the undergrowth. Who had been here and why? Had someone been wild camping? It seemed a good spot to do so, but the burn mark was long and thin, not round as you might expect with a bonfire. With the night stealthily approaching it was difficult to make much else out. I decided to return for a better look in the daylight.

Turning about once more, I nearly jumped out of my skin. Sitting on a branch at eye level, not seven feet from where I stood, was a sizeable bird staring at me with orange eyes shining like headlights. Recovering my composure, I stepped forwards for a closer look. It was a long eared owl, about a foot tall, with mottled pale and dark brown markings, with a rounded brown face and darker irises.

"Hoo-ooo. Hoo hoo," it called softly.

"Hoo-ooo, hoo hoo," I repeated, and it gazed at me through solemn eyes.

I smiled. "You're a handsome beastie," I said.

"I'm sorry if I disturbed you, although it's a bit early for you to be up and about yet, isn't it?"

The owl made no response, not so much as a blink. I nodded at it. "Go in peace," I murmured out of habit, the blessings I'd been taught as a child. "Live a long and blessed life."

I walked slowly and quietly passed its tree, holding my breath, afraid of scaring it. I half expected it to take flight but it remained where it was, feathers unruffled, no sense of alarm. Once I was well clear, I speeded up, intent on reaching the inn before dark. I hadn't travelled more than a hundred metres when the wiry vibration of the air told me my owl friend had finally taken to wing and was following me through the woods. I watched as he landed on the branch of a tree ten metres away, sitting like a sentinel, observing me as I followed the path home.

Once more, I slowed down as I passed him, and this time his head swivelled as I went by, observing my progress.

The whole process was repeated the entire journey, until finally I came to the edge of Speckled Wood. The inn, dark and quiet lay in front of me. It appeared sinister from this angle, the police tape fluttering in a gentle breeze. A scene not for the faint-hearted that was for sure. Why hadn't I left a light on? I was scaring myself.

I turned about and gazed back into the wood. My owl friend remained in plain sight, observing me.

"I have to go in," I told it, regret in my tone, surprisingly sad to be losing this odd but compelling companionship. There was no-one waiting for me inside the inn. I would be all alone. I hadn't realised this would bother me until I understood how much the owl's unexpected company had meant. Now I felt my solitude keenly. Maybe I should have remained at The Hay Loft for a few more nights, among people, however odd or rude they were.

No, that would have meant giving in. The inn was my home.

"Thank you for your company," I said to the owl. "Goodnight."

I slipped out of its sight, knowing it would remain in the woods. Perhaps I would see it again the next time I walked there.

I hoped so.

I stuffed myself with cheese and tomato sandwiches as I had promised myself I would, and then feeling a little better opted to run a bath. The bath in my private quarters was a large Victorian style tub located directly under the window, horribly scarred but wonderfully deep with enormous stiff taps that required two hands to turn. The boiler had been heating up water since the electricity had been restored earlier in the day, so there was plenty for me. I rummaged in one of my bags to find some luxurious scented bubble bath I'd been gifted at Christmas, along with a 12 pack of tea lights. I lit some of the tea lights and stood them on the window sill out of harm's way.

Slipping into the bath I luxuriated in wallowing. It had been an eventful day and my thoughts mulled over the encounters with Talbot-Lloyd and Pimm - those not entirely pleasant - but also Charity, Rhona, Stanley, Gilchrist, Millicent, Jasper and the beautiful owl. They had breathed new life into me. I considered my desire for company. *Am I lonely?* I asked myself, and frowned. Perhaps a little. I had a few friends back in London, and I'd dated from time to time in the past, but the elusive perfect companion seemed to have passed me by.

Idly, I drew a large love heart in the steam on the

window, and then, remembering a love spell from my early years, I giggled and wrote my initials on one half. AMD. In the centre of the heart I drew a plus sign. After that I was stumped. I didn't have any initials to add. There was no-one to call upon, no-one to bewitch, even if my powers were of use.

I drew a question mark instead, and then closed my eyes and inhaled the fragrant steam from the bath until my mind was clear. Opening my eyes once more and with a wry smile at the question mark, I intoned in a low voice, "Here as I cleanse my body, I call upon the gods and goddesses to help me sluice the negativity of my past away. Fill me with joy and expectation of a nurturing future. May heads turn my way; may I find the ones I wish to stay."

Then with slightly more force: "I am blessed in this world. I choose to love myself and others. I will love, I am loving, I am loved. I am love!"

Opening the window wide to allow the steam to escape, I envisaged sending my love into the world. Done with the spell I collapsed back into the water, watching steam from my body curl up and drift outside. It was pleasant to feel the cooler night breeze on my hot skin. I closed my eyes and floated away, until a sudden scratching on the window sill jerked me back to reality.

I stared in shock at the long-eared owl as it observed me with curiosity through the open window, this pink creature floundering around in the now-tepid water.

"Hoo? Hoo? Hoo?" it asked.

Chapter Eight

I awoke feeling far more positive than I had the previous afternoon, but this new positivity didn't last long. The post brought the results of the survey and Pimm appeared to be telling me that the inn required underpinning and structural work that was likely to run into hundreds of thousands of pounds. I just couldn't see it myself.

In addition, I received a huge box file from Penelope Quigwell with a backlog of bills, paperwork and instructions on how to pay. Bills were owing for maintenance to the cottages in the town, the post office and the convenience store. Nothing appeared to have been paid out by the estate for a very long time.

Feeling inordinately cross, I sat at the desk in my office and pored over the ledgers trying to make sense of money coming in and money going out. What I needed were some excel spreadsheets to keep track of it all, or an accountant. The latter sounded favourable to me. Sorting the finances would make my head explode. Even a cursory look at the figures suggested that I was haemorrhaging money from the estate faster than I was making it. If I didn't turn things around quickly, I'd be liable for bankruptcy before I fully unpacked my bags.

What on earth was I paying Hawke, Joplin and Harrow for, if they couldn't balance the books and look after the estate in my father's absence? And what about Penelope Quigwell? How much were here fees? And did she have a copy of my father's will? I hadn't even seen that. It might be worth examining just to see how well the estate had been managed since his death.

I glowered at my mobile, considering where to start. A phone call to Jason, followed by a phone call to Penelope seemed the wisest course of action. A fact-finding mission. But all the while I was dealing with admin, I couldn't be stripping wallpaper or getting the inn back into shape. I desperately needed help, but the teams of builders, painters, plumbers and electricians that I had initially envisaged, rapidly evaporated as the full nature of my financial dilemma became apparent.

Absently I pulled at a strip of wallpaper on the wall. I loved the way it came away so easily, torn from the plaster in one long strip, disclosing the smooth surface beneath. I wiggled my thumb nail under another edge and pulled again, peeling the paper away and dropping it to the floor. Within fifteen minutes I had stripped the entire wall next to my desk. The shredded paper lay at my feet, specks of paint scattered across the bare wooden floor like dandruff.

I sighed.

I'd have to clean that up now. Procrastination felt better than financial planning.

Becoming aware of someone whistling tunefully outside, I moved to the open window to investigate. I speculated that the police had arrived to resume investigations out the back, but there were no cars. A lone man dressed in jeans and a red t-shirt walked up the drive, glancing up at the building with open curiosity.

He ventured inside without invitation, and was tapping at the wall opposite the door when I found him. The main door was standing open. I tended to leave it this way, because there was nothing worth stealing and I appreciated being able to air the building in the fine weather, after all, the inn had been shut up for far too long.

Who did he think he was?

"Good morning," I bristled. "Can I help you at all?"

He turned to me, and my heart made a little flutter, instantly dousing the flames of my annoyance. He was tall, about six foot two, and muscular, with short black hair and eyes of cornflower blue, and attractive, although not in a magazine model type way. If you studied him closely, you could see his face appeared slightly asymmetrical, his lips a little too full. I could tell his nose had been broken at some point, and yet to me, the flaws made him all the more interesting.

I flushed a little and smoothed down the front of the old dress I had thrown on, worried what he would think of my round belly and overly generous hips, dusty face, and wayward hair caught up in a lazy ponytail on the back of my head.

"You're Alfhild?" he asked. "Millicent sent me."

"Alf," I said, flushing even more. What on earth was going on? Then, confused I asked, "Millicent sent you, because...?"

"She said you needed help." He smiled—and when he did, the world seemed a brighter place—and stuck out his hand. "I'm Jed Bailey. I'm a builder by trade, but a kind of odd job bod in these parts. I can turn my hand to painting, decorating, a bit of plumbing. The only thing I don't really do is electricity."

"Wow," I said, impressed, shaking his hand. It dwarfed mine. "You sound like the kind of saviour I desperately need." But could I afford it though? I thought of the list of bills languishing on my desk.

He read my mind. "I'm affordable."

"Ha! Am I that transparent?" My face always gave me away.

"Millicent said you had taken on a huge task here. It'll be worth it in the end."

"It may suck my entire inheritance down the pan."

"Yeah, I can imagine it's going to take a load of cash. I'm happy to help though. And look. I tell you what. I'm a sucker for these old places, and Whittle Inn means a lot to many of the old local folk around here. I can help out here and there between the other jobs I have, while you get on your feet. And you can add to the workforce when you can afford it."

"That's so kind," I said, and my eyes filled with tears at this unexpected generosity. I hadn't realised I was feeling so emotional.

"Is it a deal then?" He politely ignored my sudden loss of control.

"Deal!" I replied and we shook hands again.

"Good, then why don't you show me around?"

We started in the attic and worked down. Jed raised his eyebrows at the sheer amount of junk taking up space in the loft, but like me, was pleased the roof was in such good shape. On the next two floors, he agreed that we were mainly looking at painting and decorating and perhaps redoing the plumbing and tiling in the bathrooms.

I showed him my office and living quarters. Again, most of what needed to be done here was cosmetic, with perhaps a few replacement windows.

The majority of the work needed to be done in all the downstairs areas, with a deep clean undertaken in the store rooms and the kitchen, and instalment of replacement kitchen equipment where needed.

"I'd somehow like access to the outside too," I finished explaining my plans to Jed. "At the moment you can only get through to the back garden if you go directly through the kitchen, or walk around the outside of the building, but I won't want the guests doing that."

"Hmm," Jed responded thoughtfully. "Maybe you could knock through to one of the store rooms." He led me back into the bar area where I had seen him tapping on a wall earlier.

"Look." He rapped against the wall with his knuckles.

"It sounds hollow," I said in surprise.

"That's because it is. This is a partition of some kind."

"Will it go through to the store rooms behind?" I tried to conjure up an image of the floor plan in my mind.

"There's only one way to find out," Jed replied and winked. "The next time I come, I'll bring my tools and we'll have a look."

"Great. When will that be?" I tried not to appear too eager, but failed miserably.

"Well," Jed drawled. "I have a job on tomorrow." I had to hide my disappointment. "But I'm keen to find out what lurks beyond this wall myself." His eyes danced. "Why don't I come on over after I'm done, late tomorrow afternoon?"

"Perfect," I said, cursing my flushing cheeks. "I'll supply refreshments."

CHAPTER NINE

It had been a while since I'd entertained a member of the opposite sex in any capacity. The following lunchtime found me walking into the village, primarily to post numerous letters and pay a few bills at the post office, but also in search of something interesting to cook for supper.

Rhona greeted me like a long-lost friend and together we examined the vegetables, neatly displayed in baskets outside her shop. "Is your kitchen up and working properly, already?" she asked as I picked out fresh carrots, hoping they were as sweet as they looked.

"Oh Rhona. If you could see the state of it," I lamented. "It's not so much that things aren't working, it's more that it doesn't look like it's been cleaned in about thirty years. It's revolting. I've scraped off the grease from one of the cookers and I'm using that to cook on, but it makes my skin crawl to go in there. Plus, the dead man was found just outside the kitchen door."

"Ew," Rhona shuddered. "Doesn't that freak you out? It would me."

I shook my head, "No. I have to be honest. The dead don't bother me."

I turned my attention to the available fruit, and scowled disdainfully at skinny stalks of rhubarb. Someone had been forcing their fruit. It wouldn't taste as sweet as rhubarb that came later in the season. I looked up at Rhona to make that observation, and over her shoulder spotted Talbot-Lloyd heading into The Hay Loft. "They don't bother me as much as some members of the living do, that's for sure."

Rhona followed my gaze, spotted Talbot-Lloyd and sniffed. "I get what you mean," she said.

We watched him disappear and I grunted. "Mind you, I would like to know *why* this person at the inn was killed."

"What the motive was?"

"Yes."

The tinkling of a bicycle bell disturbed my thoughts. "Good afternoon, Rhona," a woman shouted from across the road, pulling up outside the village hall. Clad in a pale blue summer dress with a straw hat trimmed with the same colour ribbon, she leapt off her bicycle and waved cheerily. Easily in her sixties, she looked a picture of English perfection, posing beneath the pastel bunting hanging around the doors and windows.

"Afternoon Sally," Rhona called back, and we watched as Sally locked her bicycle to the bench and disappeared inside the community centre.

"There's a WI sale in the Hall this afternoon," Rhona said.

"WI?"

"Women's Institute. You ought to have a wander over and see what they've got. Millicent makes some astounding pasta sauces. I have no idea what she puts in them but they taste ... magical."

"Pasta sauce?" I said. "That's a great idea." Something quick and easy to do would give me more time to chat to—or help out—Jed.

"And there will be cakes," Rhona said. "The most amazing cakes."

"I'm sold!"

And I was.

Clutching a bag full of Rhona's fresh vegetables, I made my way across to the village hall. I was struck immediately by the level of noise. I could hardly hear myself think. Groups of women were gathered together, laughing, talking and exclaiming.

At the side of the large room were tables overloaded with all manner of homegrown, or home produced, produce. I spied Millicent nibbling on a slice of cake next to her own laden table. There were jams and pickles, knitted items, lace and even wood turned gifts. To my left, the kitchen area was open and teas were being served. As Rhona had promised there were cakes galore on the counter. Some whole, some sliced. It looked like paradise to a sweet toothed cake eating professional, such as myself.

Sally smiled broadly as I made my way further into the room, and stepped away from her circle. "Hello," she said, in a quintessential English accent, with clipped vowels. It was easy to deduce, she rather well-to-do. "We haven't met. I'm Sally. You're new to the area, aren't you?"

"Yes," I replied, "I'm Alf. I'm the new owner of the inn."

"Whittle Inn?" asked Sally, her face a picture of surprise. "Yes of course, I'd heard there was a new owner. Well, I'm pleased to meet you, Alf. Let me introduce you to some of your neighbours." She ushered me firmly towards a group of women, and proudly announced who I was to them. For the next ten minutes I was bombarded with questions about the inn and about the body I'd found. Numerous times I had to explain I didn't know who the man had been, and that no, I wasn't scared to live there alone.

Finally, I extricated myself and joined Millicent, sitting by her table, supping a cup of tea, and crushing the crumbs of cake left on her plate with her forefinger. She looked up at me with amusement. "I see you've made some new friends," she said and I laughed.

"Apparently so. They're all dying for a story but I'm afraid I've nothing exciting to share with them."

"Trust me, in comparison with some of the mundane lives these women are living, you're a celebrity in their circles."

"Oh dear," I said. "I hate to disappoint."

"Then don't," Millicent replied and eyed me shrewdly. "Have you decided to make a go of the inn?"

"Not one hundred per cent. But I haven't given up yet."

"Good, because that would be a tragedy."

I nodded and examined her wares. She had jars full of sauces, some were smooth, some had bits in them, and they came in a kaleidoscope of colours, red, orange, yellow and brown, and one particularly lurid green one. "These are your pasta sauces?" I asked.

"Yes. You can choose between tomato, tomato and basil, tomato and mushroom, tomato and onion, green pepper and herb, and tomato and pepper. Do you have a preference?"

"Which do you recommend?" I asked, grabbing my purse.

"I'd suggest tomato and basil and add your own vegetables," Millicent said, nodding at my bag of goodies from across the road. "But do go steady with the onion. Jed doesn't like onions in too large a quantity."

I raised my eyebrows. "He told you he was coming over?" I asked and Millicent laughed.

"Nothing escapes me, my dear. I like to keep my ear to the ground."

When I left the hall, Sally was outside unlocking her bicycle. She smiled at me as I hefted my load of vegetables and Millicent's jar of pasta sauce, whilst balancing a lemon cake with an ice glaze in the bag in my right hand.

"Did you find everything you needed?" she trilled, with the exact same tone as her bicycle bell.

"I reckon so," I said. I turned for home, and she fell in beside me, pushing the bike between us.

"You're very brave to stay at Whittle Inn, in spite of all that has gone on there." This was becoming a familiar refrain.

"All?" I asked.

"Well, you know with the murder ..."

"We're not entirely sure it was a murder though, are we?" I said. "The police are looking into it, but there was no obvious cause of death. Not the last time they spoke to me, anyway."

"Oh indeed. Indeed," Sally said hurriedly. "You have to wait to find out, don't you?"

"In the meantime, I haven't experienced any other problems."

"Not even from the woods then?"

"The woods?" I stopped walking, switching the bag from one hand to the other. "What about them?"

"There have been lots of weird sightings there." I shook my head bemused, and Sally went on, "Odd lights after dark. Strange noises. Drivers have reported things darting out of the trees in front of their cars."

I snorted. "It's probably just wild animals. Deer maybe."

"Deer aren't green though, are they?" Sally stated, her look pointed. "And they don't shriek."

"No, to be fair, deer aren't green." I stifled a giggle, envisaging the woods full of rainbow coloured wildlife. "And no, they don't shriek as far as I know. But honestly, Sally, I haven't seen anything at all that could be described as untoward. I explored out there just the other night, and I was followed home by an owl who seemed content to pop by the inn to visit me, but apart from that, all has been quiet. Perhaps people have heard foxes. They can be scary at night."

"You could be right," Sally said, but she didn't look convinced. She regarded me once more, this time with a guarded expression. I hadn't meant to take the mick or make her feel small.

"Thank you for your concern," I said and smiled at her broadly. "I'll keep an eye out, and take special care. You must pop around some time and see what I'm up to."

She looked happier. "I'd like that," she said. "During daylight hours."

CHAPTER TEN

The afternoon had disappeared quickly and my pasta sauce, heavy with mushrooms and peppers, and light on onions, simmered gently on the stove. I had some pasta ready, only dried stuff, but good quality at that, and Rhona had even been able to furnish me with a hard block of parmesan cheese.

When I heard Jed's shout from the front door of the inn, I turned the heat right down on my sauce and dashed out to meet him in the bar area.

"Good evening." He deposited his tool box in the middle of the floor next to the four large black bin-liners full of wallpaper I'd ripped from the walls upstairs, and turned to greet me. I wore a simple dark blue dress, my hair pulled back in a scruffy ponytail, and now as he looked me up and down, I remembered the half apron I was wearing, and smoothed the material down over my hips self-consciously.

"Hi," I said, "I've been cooking!" I wiped my hands exaggeratedly on the front of my apron, and hoped against hope he would mistake the pink of my cheeks with a flush from slaving over hot pots and steaming pans in the kitchen.

"I'm glad you haven't been idle while I've been at work all day," Jed replied with a wink. He wore a checked shirt over a paint spattered t-shirt and black jeans that had seen better days. He looked great.

"Oh not at all. Paperwork this morning. A bit of shopping ..." I grimaced and tailed off. It didn't sound particularly onerous to be fair. Not when there was so much that needed doing around the inn. "I meant to clear all the rubbish out of this room. Oh well - can I get you a drink?" I asked, hurrying to change the subject. "I have tea, coffee, juice, water ... wine?"

"Tea would be just grand. Not too milky, one sugar?"

"No problem."

"I'm going to fetch my ladders from the van, and then I'll make a start on removing this plaster board, okay?" He tapped the wall for effect.

"Yes, absolutely," I replied happily. "I'm dying to see what's beneath."

"Me too." He disappeared out the front door to his van, and I skipped back into the kitchen to boil the kettle, brew some tea and stir my tomatoey concoction.

The sauce bubbled in the pot as I agitated it gently. The heat was still too high so I lit a smaller ring and moved the pot across. If I chose ... if I was that way inclined ... if I gave in to the powers I had inherited and the skills I had learned ... I could add a dash of this and a splash of that ... and cast a love spell on Jed.

I smiled ruefully. And what would be the point? To bind someone to you at the expense of their own specific and explicit consent? There is nothing as magickal – or as powerful - as free will and intent. There is nothing as heady as natural desire. I would always allow love to blossom where it found its own way.

I poured tea, dark and strong into two mugs and spooned a teaspoon of sugar into Jed's. Checking on the sauce once more, I made my way out of the kitchen and walked down the corridor to the bar. Jed was balancing in his ladder, six or seven feet in the air, frowning as he tried to peel back the plaster board, using the claw of his hammer. Even before it happened I could see what was coming.

Jed's ladders were sturdy but the plasterboard was stubborn, requiring a great deal of coaxing. As

Jed yanked the plasterboard back, it suddenly came away in his hand, launching him into space, the ladder spinning away from his feet and clattering against the wall as he tumbled towards the ground.

I didn't even think. Standing stock still, a mug of tea in each hand, I called, "*Hnescian*," and directed a lightning bolt of energy at the bin bags full of wallpaper. Together, they slid rapidly across the wooden floorboards directly under Jed as he crashed to the ground. Not quite a Hollywood crash mat, but the best I could do under the circumstances.

Jed lay on his back, winded, the hammer still clasped in his right hand, his eyes wide with surprise and his mouth a perfect O.

Feeling slightly shaken myself, I edged towards him, and lifted the mugs in my hands. "Teas up," I said and laughed nervously.

Setting them down on the floor, I helped him up. He stood and ran a dusty hand though his dark hair. "What did you do?"

"Kicked the bags?" I tried, but I knew he wasn't buying it.

"You were nowhere near them."

"The wind then," I tried to shut down the questions but Jed's gaze was wary now.

"You made the bags move. What did you say?

Nee-sum? Nee-sun?" He made a good attempt at pronouncing the word, then shook his head in disbelief.

I sensed his sudden distrust and hated it. I had experienced this among mortals for my entire life, worse while I was younger. These days I had become adept at hiding what I was. Something in my stomach twisted. "Please," I said and held a quivering hand out, offering his drink. "Don't look at me like that."

"Like what?" He asked defensively.

"Like I'm somehow other, or lesser, or monstrous. I just can't bear it."

His face softened and he took the tea from me. "You're none of those things."

"Perhaps I am. For a very long time – most of my life - I've thought that about myself."

He straightened the ladder and lay the hammer on the first step, then with his free hand he guided me over to the bar, and the stools arranged next to it. He hauled himself up, I perched on mine, toes touching the floor, seeking a solid connection with the ground.

"I don't understand," he said quietly, looking back at the ladder. "Can you tell me about it? It seems to be upsetting for you, and I don't want to intrude, but ..." He gestured at the black bags. "Really. What was that?"

I nodded and studied the dark gold liquid in my mug. You can never truly escape who you are. You can run, but you can't hide.

"I'm a witch," I said, and it felt good to confess. Jed did a double take and when I nodded, pursed his lips.

"Yes, I am. Albeit a reluctant one. My mother was a witch, a powerful one. My father was an extraordinary wizard by all accounts."

"You're a witch?" Jed scratched his head and looked me up and down. Then whistled in surprise. "I'm ... Well ... I didn't know such things actually existed."

"We do."

Jed looked from me and back to the ladder. "I see." He laughed nervously, "And you can do ...spells?"

"By any stretch of the imagination I should be capable of great things. But I'm not. I'm like this inn. Flawed, imperfect, structurally sound but a bit of a mess. Wonky."

"You're a wonky witch?" Jed asked and I was relieved to see his eyes dance with amusement, rather than glower with accusation.

"The wonkiest," I said.

"I'm sure that's not true," Jed soothed and he reached across to take my mug from me. Setting it down on the counter he took my hands in his huge ones.

"It is though." I basked in his warm grasp.

"How can you say that, when you just saved me from ... what could have been a serious injury?"

"I avoid ... being, doing, thinking or feeling anything remotely witchy," I replied.

"But why?" When I shrugged, Jed squeezed my hands and with a nod of his head indicated to the site of his fall once more. "You obviously aren't doing a good job of that, in my opinion."

He was trying to make me feel better, and I was glad he seemed so accepting of my news, but I had a long history of trying to avoid the inevitable. He waited for further explanation and I swallowed, unsure whether to tell him more. Under his scrutiny I decided to keep things simple. "Eighteen years ago, when I was twelve, I had a falling out with my Dad. It was only a small thing. Ridiculous. He wanted me to do my homework. I wanted to play out with a friend, or ride my bike, or something stupid. He said I could do that afterwards. But I was angry with him, and we had an argument and as a punishment he told me I couldn't go out even after I'd completed my homework."

I could remember the day as if it was yesterday. I'd cried a storm, shouted and screamed and thrown a tantrum as only a twelve-year-old can, caught as they are between childhood and early adulthood. "Then he had an appointment, and I watched him leave from my bedroom window, and as he reached the corner ... just as he turned out of my sight..."

I swallowed the huge lump in my throat. Fighting back tears I remembered my Dad walking away from me and pausing on the corner to turn back and wave to me as he often did. "I cursed him," I whispered. "I told him if I couldn't go out, he couldn't come home. And he never did. I never saw him again."

Tears rolled down my cheeks and suddenly I was sobbing, harsh, loud sobs. Memories of my heart-break in the face of my own actions all those years ago, meant the loss seemed as real and painful as it had back then. Jed slid off his stool, and wrapped his arms around me. I cried into his t-shirt, hot salty tears, bitter with remorse and self-hatred.

When I had calmed down a little, he stepped back and regarded me with concern. "You can't know for certain that what you said that night was the cause of your father's disappearance. Anything might have happened to him."

"I know," I sniffed sadly, "but certainly I feel my mother blamed me when I told her what I had done. We never heard from him again. There was no inkling of what had befallen him. But believe me, if he could have come home he would have done. I know he would have done."

Jed hugged me once more as the tears welled up again. "Since then – in spite of pressure from my mother and the Elders - I've resisted all pressures to give in to what is laughingly termed 'my calling'."

"I see." Jed stroked my back. "But it does, doesn't it? Call to you, I mean. I can tell. Everything about you, your energy, the way you look, the light in your eyes. Even now, when you're so sad ... it's magical."

"Is it?" I asked, turning my head away so he couldn't see me, ready to deny it all afresh, but Jed caught my chin in his hand and tilted my face gently.

"Yes," he said, and leaned down to kiss me gently on the lips.

It was a warm evening. We sat on the front step, both of us with a bowl of pasta balanced precariously on our knees and a glass of wine by our sides. The moon was rising in a clear sky, and the stars were popping out one by one.

"You know what I think?" Jed was saying. "This inn could be the making of you."

"It could be the death of me," I replied, forking spaghetti into my mouth as daintily as possible.

"Look at it this way. For years you've been denying who you really are. You've had no freedom to express yourself. That's not healthy for anybody."

"You sound like a psychologist or something," I said, wondering how Jed could manage to eat and talk and not spill anything down his front.

"I studied psychology at university so it's good to hear something sunk in," Jed said and laughed.

"You have a degree?" I asked incredulously. "Why are you knocking down walls for a living?"

"Well, like you, I followed the family trade."

"Unlike me you mean," I replied smartly.

Jed shook his head. "You can deny it all you want, but you've shown me today what you're capable of. If you didn't want to use the powers you have, you wouldn't have saved my bacon."

"I'm beginning to wish I hadn't," I wagged my fork at him in mock frustration.

"The thing is Alf, I really enjoy knocking down

walls and stripping paper and painting things. It suits me in a way very little else does. Taking my degree was great, but I didn't know what to do with myself afterwards. There was nothing burning a hole in me, no great passion. I drifted back to Whitlecombe to help my Dad out. I had a kind of apprenticeship with him, you could say. And here I am."

"Here you are," I repeated. "And you're happy?"

"Never happier," he beamed his sunshine smile my way. I could tell he was. He radiated quiet calm and general positivity.

We finished up the rest of the pasta quietly, until he asked, his tone light, almost delicate, "What about you? Did you have an apprenticeship of sorts?"

"To own an inn?"

"No," his voice gently mocked me, "to be a witch."

"Like Hogwarts, you mean?" I growled. He obviously wasn't going to let the subject drop, but then it was probably the most curious thing he had ever heard, so why would he?

I sighed. Tutted. Swept my long hair up in a ponytail and twirled it around, hesitating, wondering what to tell him, or how to tell him enough to satisfy him and so he'd leave me in peace.

But I didn't really want him to leave me in peace. I found his company exciting.

"Not exactly," I replied. "There were no special schools available for me, but I did attend classes the Elders ran in London during the weekends. After my father disappeared, I tried to go less often. It was a source of huge frustration for my mother, but I didn't want to exercise my magickal powers or enhance my skills in any way. I stopped going altogether as soon as I was 16 and could get away with it."

Jed nodded. "I can see why you felt you wanted to make a break from it all." He hesitated. "Does that mean that if you had carried on studying, you would have been a powerful witch? More powerful than you are now?"

I frowned, staring back through time, into my past, to the school I had attended in Somerset, and the special classes that had been held on Celestial Street. The years had made many memories dusty, and enhanced others with a false nostalgic glow. I remembered the teachers, their wise crinkled old faces, their curiosity and intelligence, their eagerness to share their own knowledge and to enhance what was already within me. Shadowmender's benevolent face swam in front of me for a moment.

I blew the air out of my lungs in one long breath,

scattering the memories. “That’s complicated,” I answered. “The thing is, witchcraft is an innate ability, but it is also something that can be learned and practised. I have the powers within me, so I can cast spells, and practise kinesis and communicate in strange ways, but I lack training in certain skills, such as potions and herblore and the like. You witnessed something very instinctive and primeval earlier. Most of what I can do comes directly from my intent. I control those basic abilities. And I keep them well hidden.”

“But in an emergency they break out?”

“It certainly appears to be that way.” I fiddled with my wine glass. Jed reached for the bottle and topped up my glass, but not his own. He was driving of course.

“What abilities do you have?”

“As you saw, moving objects. As a kid I used to play practical jokes on other people – shifting objects, hiding things in plain sight. That was a bit naughty. Oh and I loved to communicate with animals – that was fun. I can communicate with spirits too, but that can be less fun, but it does mean I’m not scared of the dark, or of the dead. That’s why I don’t mind staying here alone in the inn, in spite of the fact that everyone thinks I shouldn’t.”

"Yes, they all think you're exceptionally brave and perhaps a bit crazy in the village."

"Do they?"

"They do. But by all accounts, many of the older ones thought the same way about your father and grandmother so you're in good company."

I smiled at the thought. "That's fair enough."

"So what can't you do?"

I rolled my eyes. "If I told you that, you'd know my weaknesses." I was joking but I considered the question anyway. Where was my training lacking? "I'm not a great spellcaster. My father and mother were both incredible, although my mother rarely used spells. She said they were dangerous. That they could be put to heinous uses. So I can't curse people, and thanks to my mother, I would always be very careful about using magick for my own benefit."

"You can't make yourself wealthy then?"

"Perhaps I could, but I've never tried. You should have seen the hovel I was living in, up in London. Hospitality pays peanuts, even in our grand capital. I had a room in a house that was smaller than my mother's cottage and in a far worse state. And besides, in many ways I am wealthy now. I have this," I gestured around me at the inn.

"Huge potential."

"Me or the inn?" I smirked playfully.

"Ha ha," Jed replied and slid over on the step to sit closely to me, our hips and shoulders touching. "Definitely both. I think you'll get this place back on its feet in no time."

"I admire your confidence. I just hope I can pay the bills," I said. "And sometimes I worry that I won't be able to run it."

"You have to trust in yourself. That's half the battle."

"That's true."

"Hoo hoo," the deep timbre of an owl from close by echoed my words.

Jed almost jumped out of his skin. I placed my right hand gently on his left forearm to stop him moving too quickly. "There," I directed softly, "to your right. It's a friend of mine."

Jed peered into the gloom and did a double take when he finally spotted the owl, perching on the guttering above the bowed bay window. "Wow," he whispered. "Your friend?"

"He often visits."

"He? Do you have a name for him?"

"Why would I name him? He names himself."

"You know it's a he though?"

"Yes." I did.

"What is *his* name then?"

I shook my head. "I don't know. I haven't asked him."

"So ask him now."

Part of me obstinately wanted to refuse. I wasn't a child doing a party trick, and I didn't particularly want to show off my skills, but the other part of me was curious too.

"You ask him," I said. "But don't alarm him."

"He speaks English?"

"He speaks owl, but like I told you just now, magick is all about the intention."

Jed pursed his lips and looked at me, then back at the owl. "Hey, Mr Owl. What's your name?"

The owl's eyes flicked our way. It studied Jed warily and remained quiet. I smiled at it. "What is your name?" I asked. "I'd like to know too."

His head swivelled. "Hoo-ooo. Hoo-ooo. Hoo-ooo. Hoo-ooo."

"What did he say?" asked Jed.

"Grimbleweed Clutterbeak."

"You're pulling my leg, right?"

I laughed in delight. "He said you can call him Mr Hoo."

"Well, Mr Hoo," Jed turned back to the owl and bowed his head, "we're honoured."

"Hoo-ooo. Hoo-ooo. Hoo oooo."

"He is too," I said.

But the owl hadn't said that at all. He'd told me to take care.

Last thing that evening, I stood in front of the window staring at the woods and wondering about Mr Hoo, when my attention was grabbed by something out there. The hair on the back of my neck prickled as I stepped closer to the glass, and turned the bedside-light out in order to see better. I imagined for a moment I spotted a twirling red light in the wood, about the size and shape of a disco ball. It appeared to hover in the air for a while, before shooting backwards and disappearing under the cover of the foliage. I watched and waited, but when I didn't see it again I decided it must have been my imagination.

Nonetheless, my heart hammered in my chest for a long time before I was finally able to fall asleep, and my dreams were haunted by a man wearing a sparkling red ring.

CHAPTER ELEVEN

The following evening, we managed to bust through the false wall in the inn's main room. As Jed had surmised, the bar had one been one huge room at some stage, but had been partitioned to create store rooms next door to the kitchen. With the partition down, the bar became a large L-shape. The added bonus was finding a huge fireplace behind the plasterboard. In fact, it was so big, both Jed and I could stand where the grate would be and stare up the chimney.

"Do you think it's functioning?" I asked as Jed craned his head backwards.

"Not at the moment, but I reckon if we get someone on the roof, and a sweep down here, they'll be able to tell us."

"Do chimney sweeps still exist?" I asked, incredulous at the idea.

Jed laughed. "Yes, of course. I don't think anyone's invented a self-cleaning chimney just yet."

"Oh they have. It's called central heating." I smirked a little. "What about little chimney sweep boys?"

"Not seen since Mary Poppins."

We giggled together and stepped away from the chimney. It had been a good day's work. I had started setting up some systems on my laptop to keep an eye on finances and begun planning for work on the inn and the cottages in the village. After lunch, I had pulled more wallpaper off. I enjoyed this process – pulling layer after layer of the past away and discarding each, ready for a new start.

I shook dust out of my hair, feeling more than a little tired. "I'm sorry," I said. "It's getting on and I haven't even thought about making something to eat."

"Hey, no problem!" Jed said. "I don't expect you to cook for me just cos I'm over here in the evening."

"I know, but ..."

"No buts. Look, let's just head down to The Hay Loft and see what they have on the menu. The food can be a bit hit and miss, but you can't go too wrong with a toasted sandwich."

Reluctantly I agreed, and after a quick wash and

spruce up, I joined Jed outside. "Your carriage awaits, milady," Jed bowed, and raising my eyebrows I clambered into his beaten up van. The vehicle was old enough to start with, but the local conditions made sure it looked far worse. I imagined that driving through the lanes around Whittlecombe in anything larger than a Fiat 500, was liable to lead to the occasional prang or scratch.

The Hay Loft wasn't particularly busy so we had our choice of tables. There wasn't much to tempt my appetite on the menu *per se*, so I hovered near the unlit fire, reading through the list of specials hanging on the wall above, while Jed waited to order drinks at the bar.

I didn't need a sixth sense to realise I'd attracted someone's attention, and I turned to notice a large man with a red face glowering in the doorway. He had a German Shepherd dog on a lead, and both were regarding me in a less than friendly manner.

"Hello," I said, determined not to feel intimidated in the face of such apparent hostility.

The man sniffed and led the dog inside, disappearing behind the bar area and out of sight. Two minutes later he returned.

"Alright, Lyle?" Jed said.

"Jed." Lyle nodded, his face impassive. "What can I get you?"

"A couple of pints of Otter, please, mate. I said I'd introduce Alf here to the delights of the local brewery."

"What are you doing hanging about with her?" Lyle asked, as though I wasn't standing within hearing distance. Jed frowned. "You an item?" Lyle prompted.

"I'm doing some work for Alf. She's new here. I wanted to make her feel welcome. Is that okay?"

"Well, I don't know. Is it?"

"Lyle—"

"There's no need for competition in a place the size of Whittlecombe, is there? It's damaging for my business."

"Oh, come on, Lyle. Whittle Inn has been here for centuries. If anything it has more right to exist than The Hay Loft."

"That's as maybe, but it closed down for a reason. People want something more upmarket. They're not going to get that at Whittle Inn."

Jed opened his mouth to respond, but I nudged him. "Come on," I said. "We can sit outside."

Jed paid for the drinks and Lyle glared at me.

"That place is a death trap," he said. "It wouldn't surprise me if it burned to the ground."

I bristled with indignation, but Jed nudged me with his elbow and I followed him out to the beer garden. I could tell by the set of Jed's jaw that he was fuming too, and as soon as we found a table, he apologised.

"Oh don't be daft," I sighed. "If I had been the only inn in business for the past few years, I suppose I'd feel a tad gutted I was facing new competition too."

"He feels threatened by you."

"By my inn, yes. But I'm no threat to him. And I'm not sure the inn is, in reality."

Jed looked at me thoughtfully. "Does it make you feel bad, knowing there are people who don't want you to succeed."

"It's not the best feeling in the world, I'll admit. But I'm not doing it for them."

"Are there many here in the village who have been rude to you? People who have ..."

"Looked at me like I don't belong? Like I'm not wanted?" I bit my lip and considered my recent dealings with locals. "On the whole everybody has been welcoming. Just this Lyle character. Oh, and my surveyor was a weird one. Very unfriendly. And then there was Talbot-Lloyd. He was particularly charming."

"Enough to wish you harm?" Jed asked with concern, but I shook my head.

"Surely not. Like I said. Their bile is directed at the inn, not at me personally." I wasn't entirely convinced of this myself, remembering Talbot-Lloyd's remarks about my relative youth.

"Okay, so they may not want to harm you, but they would be pleased to see the inn languish and never re-open."

"I can't know that for sure."

"The murder ..."

"We can't assume it was a murder, we don't know the facts yet."

"But it's a possibility," Jed insisted. "Someone may have left a body on your back step as a message. Maybe they want you to think twice about opening the inn."

Of course, the thought had crossed my mind.

"Let's not jump to conclusions," I reiterated. "When the police have something concrete to tell me, I'm sure they'll let me know."

The encounter with Lyle left a bad taste in my mouth, so it was no wonder that I spent half the night awake with indigestion. Sometime around three in the morning, I hauled myself blearily out of bed to visit the bathroom. The light of the moon illuminated my surroundings so I didn't bother with a light, but I nearly jumped out of my skin when a pale face bobbed into view, and I realised there was a woman standing in the doorway to my bedroom. Dressed in a dark evening gown, with her hair elaborately coiled around her head, she seemed vaguely familiar.

"Did I startle you?" she asked as my shriek died away.

"Just a bit! How did you get in here?" I backed towards the bed, feeling for my dressing gown.

She looked around puzzled. "Through the front door, I imagine. I can't remember."

"You can't remember?"

"It was some time ago."

"You can't just walk around my home without a by-your-leave." I pulled my robe around me and tightened the cord.

"Your home?" The woman's tone turned haughty. "I think you'll find this is my home."

I took another look at what she was wearing and

the paleness of her skin, and realised exactly what had happened.

"You can't be here," I said obstinately.

"What do you mean? Clearly I can be here, because I am. It is you who shouldn't be here."

"You're a ghost," I said.

"Absurd," the woman retorted, dancing further into the room.

"I didn't summon you so *you* should not be here," I tried to explain as kindly as I could.

Kindness didn't cut her mustard. "What an outrage! *I* did not summon *you*. *You're* the ghost and *you* are the one who should not be here. And sleeping in *my* bed." She drew herself up to her full height and glared at me, her dark eyes sparkling.

I opened my mouth to protest and then closed it again. Her bed? Had she been planning on sleeping here? With me?

I reached out a tentative hand to touch her, but my fingers found only air.

"Look around," I said. "What do you see? Do you see your room as it should be?"

The woman tutted and whirled around, her skirts flying. "Yes. Yes. Of course." But then she faltered. I watched as she moved to the edge of the room and examined where I had peeled the wallpaper away. "What's the meaning of this? Did you do this? I had that paper hand painted by a Chinese artist. It was *very* expensive." She scowled my way before taking a few steps sideways. "And where is my dresser?"

In frustration, she rounded on me. "What is the meaning of this? I'll call Lulubelle and have you removed." She reached for something, perhaps a pull for a bell that might once have brought a servant running, but that was long gone. She paused, her hand in the air, staring at me with sudden fear. "It's gone. Everything has changed. Except the bed. That's the same. In the same place."

"I'm sorry," I said softly. I wasn't sure, but I imagined it might be tough to find out you're both dead and a ghost.

"Oh," she said and her shoulders sagged. "I've been awake for so long. I'm feeling so tired. I just wanted to lie down."

"You can lie here," I indicated the bed. "Make yourself at home. I'll be back in a minute."

She stepped past me and sat on the bed. I closed the door of the en suite bathroom, and when I opened it again, she had gone.

The next morning, before breakfast, I headed up to the attic and the paintings I'd found there. On the top of the pile was the portrait of the woman who had visited me in the night. I recognised her instantly by the elaborate coils of braids wrapped tightly on her head. She was an imposing looking woman, not someone you would want to mess with, but even so, there was a vulnerability in her eyes. I dragged the frame out from beneath the sheet and gave her a quick wipe with a duster. At the foot of the frame was a small gold plaque bearing the legend 'Alfhild Gwynfyre Daemonne'. With a rush of emotion, I realised this had to be my great grandmother.

I felt sad about the encounter, and wished I'd had more time to talk to her. This proved, as I'd suspected, that the ghosts of my ancestors did indeed walk the halls of Whittle Inn. If I wanted to, I could summon them to keep me company.

But why would I want to? I had no need of ghosts or witchcraft. I was fine the way I was.

Chapter Twelve

Hearing a car pull up on the gravel drive outside the inn later that day, I thought nothing of it, expecting Jed to arrive at any moment. It was a surprise therefore when I trotted down the now completely carpetless stairs to come face to face with Detective Gilchrist.

"Hi," I greeted him. "Do you have news?"

He smiled to see me covered in sawdust and flecks of dry paint. I'd been attempting to sand down the doors in my office, but given the sheer number of layers of old paint and varnish I figured I was going to require some super-sanding machine of some kind.

"I do have news after a fashion. Is there somewhere we can sit?"

Deciding it wouldn't be the done thing to invite a detective to take a seat on the front step, I led him towards the bar and the stools that had taken up residence there. He perched, and gazed across at the empty bar area behind me. Jed and I had stripped back the plasterboard and revealed the old mirrors. It looked much like a proper old pub now. "I feel as though I should be ordering a drink," Gilchrist said.

"Coffee would be the best I can manage today," I replied, turning for the kitchen but Gilchrist stopped me.

"No, no, I'm fine, thanks. Not long had one."

"Okay. Well hopefully the inn will be up and running in a few months and you'll be able to order a drink for real. I'll invite you to the opening do."

"That will be great. I'll be here."

"Excellent." I hopped up on my stool next to him. "So what can I do for you?"

"We've had the results of the post-mortem back from our victim. The results are inconclusive, so I'm afraid I have more questions than answers."

"What does that mean?" I asked, puzzled. "That he wasn't murdered?"

"No. I think one of the conclusions we can safely draw at this time is that the gentleman didn't die a natural death. However, we're not entirely certain how he died, and we still have no further clue as to who he is."

"I see." I pondered on what Gilchrist was saying,

and also on what he wasn't telling me. I wondered how far I dared to push him for more details. "Can you give me any idea about his injuries?"

Gilchrist looked around as though he half expected someone else to walk in, and then lowering his voice he replied. "It is the strangest thing. As far as the pathologist can tell, the victim died of multiple injuries. Every single large bone in his body was fractured. As in broken. Not pulverised or crushed. And his injuries were not compatible with a fall from a height or a collision so he can't have tumbled off the roof."

I almost fell from my stool.

"Are you alright, Ms Daemonne?" Gilchrist asked with concern.

"Percussive shock," I said but I knew he wouldn't know what that meant.

"Sorry?" Gilchrist asked and I shook my head, my knees and elbows feeling decidedly wobbly.

"There was no bruising to the body?" I asked.

"None at all. Which is highly unusual given the nature of the rest of his injuries."

Gilchrist studied me curiously. "Oh," I said, because he appeared to be waiting for me to elucidate. I was at a loss. How could I tell him of my certainty that what he was describing was the work of a witch or a wizard. Most likely a dark warlock. Black magic. That put a whole new spin on the dangers lurking in and around the inn.

"You haven't seen anything unusual in the time you've been here?" asked Gilchrist, poised over his phone, ready to make notes.

"No, nothing."

"Have you had many visitors?"

"A few."

"People you know?"

"Well, no. Not really. I mean ... I know them now." Gilchrist nodded his encouragement, obviously wanting me to list them. "Let me see. There was the surveyor, Charles Pimm. Millicent Ballicott from the village. Stanley Marsh from the village shop. Jed Bailey. He's an odd job man who's doing some work for me."

"And you haven't seen anyone hanging around, or acting in a suspicious way?"

"No."

"Only we've had a few reports about strange lights and noises from the woods behind the inn and wondered if you'd seen or heard anything?"

Sally. I rolled my eyes. "Green deer?" I said and it was Gilchrist's turn to look puzzled. I stifled a nervous giggle. "Honestly, I've seen and heard nothing at all."

"And no-one's made any threats against you or the inn?"

Now I hesitated. I thought of Lyle at The Hay Loft and Talbot-Lloyd, but both had been miserable and belligerent rather than overtly threatening. I had no real grounds for complaint, so I smiled and said, "No. Nothing."

Gilchrist flipped the cover on his mobile across its face. "Thanks, Ms Daemonne. That's all for now. If you do think of anything you will let me know?"

"Yes of course."

"Would it be alright if I just had another quick look around the back?"

"No problem. I'll let you out." I led him past the bar and down the corridor with The Snug and The Nook beyond, then we walked through the kitchen to the back door. He watched in satisfaction as I slid the bolts open top and bottom and then twisted the keys in the pair of locks. "Good security," he said and I smiled, "It's just a shame you leave the front door wide open most of the time."

We walked out onto the slabbed area and he examined the general area again, snapping a few photos with his mobile, before spending some time craning his head to look up at the upstairs windows and the roof above them. Given that a fall would have resulted in a completely different set of injuries, and there was nothing out here that could have caused the injuries that Gilchrist had described to me, I figured the detective was on a hiding to nothing.

Eventually he sighed deeply, obviously no closer to an answer. "Thanks for your time, Ms Daemonne." I walked him through the inn to the front door. As I watched him drive off, I shivered. It was a warm afternoon, but suddenly I could sense danger in the breeze. I was alone again, and now it seemed I didn't simply have to worry about Talbot-Lloyd, Lyle and their ilk, I had dark magick to fear too.

A little later Jed arrived, and finding the front door closed, had to bang hard to get my attention. "What's happened?" he asked, his face lined with concern when I finally made it downstairs and drew back the bolts.

"I'm a little unnerved," I said, leading Jed through to the kitchen. "Detective Gilchrist came over to ask a few more questions, and fill me in on what the police have found out."

"And what have they found out?"

I frowned, wondering how much I could share with Jed, but I desperately wanted to confide in someone.

"It's not really what they know," I faltered as I reached for the kettle to fill it at the sink. "More what they don't know or could ever possibly understand."

"How do you mean?" Jed grabbed a pair of mugs and the teapot.

"It's the manner in which the unknown man died. Gilchrist described how all of the major bones in the body were broken."

"So he fell?" Jed speculated. "From the roof of the inn, to the patio area outside."

"No. He can't possibly have fallen because he had no other traumatic injuries."

"What then?"

"You'll think this is crazy ... but I think it was a spell. I think he was cursed. Possibly using the Curse of Madb."

"Maeve?"

"Yes. Madb was a Celtic Goddess, a great hedonist and war-mongerer. She was known to covet the possessions of others and wage war to get her hands on what she wanted."

"So someone cursed the victim because they wanted what he had?"

"That's a possibility, but it doesn't make sense. It's more likely that the victim was envious of, or was coveting the inn, or something in these parts. The Curse of Madb is used *against* those who have an appetite to defraud someone or steal from them."

"You're right. That does sound crazy. Why do you think this is the case?"

"Because the injuries that Gilchrist described sound like percussive shock to me." When Jed looked even more puzzled, I expanded. "Think of the way a shrill or loud noise can break glass. That's effectively what the Curse of Madb does. It causes a shock to the bones. Multiple fractures, sudden and complete organ failure. No other injuries. It's highly effective. Death is swift and painless. Apparently."

"Apparently?" Jed gulped.

"I've never seen it in practice. It's something that can only be performed by extremely powerful spell-casters."

"You can't do it?"

"I've never tried, and I would be unlikely to ever do it anyway. Very few witches would."

"Why wouldn't you ever use it?"

"Do you remember what I said about using magick with intent? Well, that's the way you cast a spell. The same word, or curse, can have different meanings depending on the level of intent used. The point being that it is possible to use a milder version of the Curse of Madb simply as a spell to stop someone. Momentarily freeze them in their tracks if you like. You don't have to go the whole hog and take someone out. Just a little intonation, and a sprinkling of mild intent, those will do the job."

"You're saying that—" Jed struggled to get his head around what I was trying to tell him.

"I'm saying that anyone who is a powerful enough spellcaster, could have simply stopped this guy in his tracks without having to kill him. The fact that he was killed suggests either there's a rogue force at work – be that witch, wizard, warlock or whomever—or ..."

"Or?"

"Or whatever this chap was up to, it was serious enough to make the perpetrator very angry indeed."

Jed nodded.

"I wasn't particularly worried about this murder before. I felt somehow disconnected from it. Maybe I assumed it was some weird random act or accident, that predated my arrival here. If only by hours. But now I am definitely worried." I absently stirred my tea. "But this ... It's too close to home and makes me think that the inn is under serious threat by persons known or unknown." I stared at Jed, my brow furrowing. "Maybe someone exacted revenge against somebody who is coveting the inn or my inheritance, or maybe the person that killed the man here is determined to harm the inn's reputation. Whatever," I took a deep swallow of my tea, "I'm at a loss to know whether it's my kind or your kind I need to keep an eye on."

"My kind?" Jed looked nervous.

"I don't know whether it's magick or mortals that threaten my livelihood."

Chapter Thirteen

The inn was a virtual shell now compared to how it had been when I'd first arrived. Jed and I knocked through partition after partition, or stripped off yards of plaster board. It was dusty, unforgiving work, and back-breaking to carry all the endless rubbish out to the skip I'd hired. The dust wafted through the inn endlessly, and I gazed in despair at how it layered and coated every surface, even when the doors had been closed and the gaps between the floor and door lagged.

"I'll never feel clean again," I lamented, wondering about the price of hiring cleaning staff in the area. How much would it cost to deep clean the entire inn? I couldn't dare start plastering or painting with this much dust throughout the building.

The good news was that every time I peeled back

another false wall, I found new treasures underneath. Beautifully ornate fireplaces in the bedrooms, exquisite panelling in both The Snug and The Nook, and behind the bar we found more beautiful carved wood and shelving along with the Victorian mirrors, dappled and scarred through years of use and abuse, but totally salvageable. Jed was quick to cover them up once more, intent on protecting them until we were ready to proceed with the refurbishment of the bar area.

We were progressing, that was true enough, but I found myself increasingly on edge most of the time. I figured that if someone were watching either me or the inn, I would instinctively know it, and in truth, there were times when I found myself turning in circles and looking around with suspicion, but I could never sense anything malevolent.

Far from it. The deeper I scratched at the surface of the inn, the more I uncovered its filthy dusty layers, and the more the inn appeared to breathe with relief. It was as if the inn had been wound as tight as a spring over the centuries, and now, by exposing the beams and the original brickwork - and even wattle and daub in a few places - I was helping it to regain a sense of self.

Perhaps it had lost its way as much as I had. This was our chance. Mine to find a life for myself that had meaning, and the inn's to finally come fully back to life.

I was determined we would be successful. Whatever it took.

To that end, later that night after Jed had finished up and headed home in his battered van, and with Mr Hoo looking on in solemn interest, I sat on the step, peeled off my shoes and cleared my mind, preparing for a protection ritual.

That morning I had received an anonymous note in the post. The contents were straightforward enough. Just seven little words: *Leave now before we force you out.*

I had turned the note over and over in my hands, but apart from the fact that it had been written on good quality cream parchment, it didn't appear to hold any further clues. I'd taken a few photos and attached them to a text for Detective Gilchrist, and promised to save the envelope and contents until the next time I saw him.

For now, I needed to concentrate on protecting myself and the inn.

I had been mentally preparing myself all day,

and now that I was alone, it was time. Calling upon the goddess Bast, I walked barefoot around the perimeter of my property in the largest circle I could manage. I began at the gate and proceeded all the way around the inn and back to the start, right around the external footprint of the building. In the absence of a bell to use, I clapped my hands as I went, repeating the phrase, '*Guard this space from all ill will and all those who wish us harm.*' Over and over I repeated the phrase, planting my feet squarely on the earth, alternately feeling the sandy soil beneath my toes, or the coolness of concrete depending on where I was walking. The next time I circumnavigated the property I sprinkled salt water in front of me to represent earth and water. It splashed my legs, and left streaks in the dust.

Finally, I lit three sticks of incense to represent fire and air and carried them with me, scenting the air with a musky eastern promise and this time I concentrated on the idea of positivity and purity, keeping anything less than wholesome at bay, while visualising an impenetrable mountain fortress.

When I had completed the ritual, I thanked Bast and sank onto the front step of the inn thankfully. Mr Hoo fluttered down to sit next to me.

"Hooo-oo. Hoo-oooo," he told me, the light shining bright in his beautiful eyes.

"Yes, you're right," I replied. "We've done what we can for now, but we'll still need to keep watch for anything unusual or anyone that wishes us harm." We sat together listening to the sounds of the night, in contemplative but companionable silence.

CHAPTER FOURTEEN

Having wandered down into the village to send a few letters from the post office, and fully intending to pick up a few things from Rhona's little shop, I decided to make time for coffee and a slice of cake. The little tea shop in Whittlecombe was a refuge of civility and calm, with tables covered in red and white chequered cloths, and old-fashioned dressers laden down with china and knick-knacks, lining the walls.

I took a table by the window, perfect for people watching, and ordered a cream tea from the waitress, a pleasant old woman named Gloria, who had probably worked in the café since time immemorial. Her long hair, as white as snow, was teased to perfection and drawn up in an impressive beehive. She had secured this magnificent style in place with enough metal grips to recreate the Eiffel Tower, and enough hairspray to turn the café into an inferno if she walked near an open flame. I gave her my order and watched with some trepidation as she hobbled away on her thick ankles and ultra-sensible shoes.

While waiting for my refreshments, I pulled a number of documents from my bag that needed attention. Now the initial panic over my finances had passed, and I'd set up spreadsheets and scoured all the financial information relating to the accounts for the inn and the cottages that the estate administered, I was in a much better place and able to see where I was and what needed to be spent where.

Penelope Quigwell had furnished me with all the information I had asked for, but now as I scanned through the documents, I could see a number of large gaps in the accounting dating from my father's disappearance that still hadn't been taken into consideration despite several previous requests. I hoiked my mobile out of my bag and rang her office. The dour gentleman receptionist answered and haughtily informed me Penelope was out of the office visiting clients for the next few days but he would let her know I had been trying to reach her.

I made a note in my diary to follow it up. Getting

information from Penelope was proving trying to say the least. I considered the option of returning to London briefly. I could call into her office, pick up some supplies from the shops in Celestial Street, and organise for the rest of my belongings to be sent down here to the inn, all at the same time. It would make a nice change, time well spent, and give me a break from renovating all day, every day.

As Gloria returned with a tray full of delicious items, I hurriedly swept my paperwork and phone from the table and dumped it on the chair next to me. Gloria carefully balanced the tea tray on the edge of the table, and set down a teapot covered in a bright red hand knitted woollen tea cosy, a cup and saucer in pale cream with rainbow coloured polka dots, a matching plate laden with two beautifully fluffy fruit scones, a huge bowl of clotted cream and a slightly smaller bowl of homemade strawberry jam.

I dribbled my thanks and set to with gusto. One scone would have sufficed, but two was pushing it a little. I probably wouldn't need to eat again for a fortnight.

I was just finishing up the second scone and ruminating on the left over clotted cream—such a shame to waste it—when Millicent came into the café and waved at me cheerily. "I spotted you through the window," she sang, "and thought I'd enquire how you're getting on."

"Hello," I said, "come and sit with me."

"Are you sure? I wouldn't want to intrude."

"No, it's nice to have the company."

Gloria hobbled over as Millicent settled into her seat, and we ordered more tea. "Speaking of company," Millicent said, "how are you and Jed getting on?"

"Oh," I flushed, "very well."

Millicent raised her eyebrows. "That well, eh? Interesting." When I glanced at her, she smiled, "I'm glad. He's a lovely young man."

I laughed, a little self-consciously. "We're just friends, Millicent," I said, and that much was true, although I often found myself thinking of him when he wasn't around. "Thanks for the recommendation. Really. Jed's worth his weight in gold. We're making great progress on stripping the inn back. I've already had to send off three skips full of rubbish since he started working with me."

"Excellent."

"Jed's making a start on sanding the paintwork back wherever possible, with his super-loud but highly efficient sanding machine, and he suggested we get all of the doors dipped and stripped, so eventually when we rehang them, they'll be as close to original as possible. I'm looking forward to that."

"It will all take shape in good time," Millicent said. She removed the tea cosy from the teapot and lifted the lid, stirring the tea inside and checking the colour, until it was to her satisfaction.

"How's everything else up there?" she asked and watched me as I replied.

"It's all ... fine," I said.

"No other problems?" she asked and I shook my head.

"No."

"That's good. Have you seen the news today?" she asked.

"The news?"

"The local newspaper is running a story on the man that was found at your inn. They have an artist's impression. The police are trying to discover who he is."

"Do you have a copy?" I asked, curious to see the likeness.

"No, I have my papers delivered so I was reading about it at home this morning. Rhona will have plenty though."

"Yes." Of course she would.

"Did the police talk to you again?"

"Detective Gilchrist came to see me," I said.

"It's such a strange thing to have happened, isn't it?" Millicent asked conversationally. "Of course, Whittle Inn always had a bit of a reputation for attracting some rather eccentric characters?"

"Did it?" I asked, genuinely interested in the history of the inn, of which I knew relatively little. "What sort of eccentric characters?"

Millicent looked around to make sure we weren't being overheard, and then made a swivelling motion with her finger, to include me and herself in some sort of secret circle.

"Our sort," she said in a low voice.

"Witches?" I clarified.

"Yes, of all persuasions and flavours."

"Mad, bad and dangerous to know? That kind of thing?"

"Oh indeed," Millicent giggled. "I told you I used to visit the inn to play with your father when I was a girl? Why I remember some very dashing wizards from back in your father's youth. They could turn a young girl's head. But then there were the very sinister ones, the dark witches and wizards, and some incredibly disturbing warlocks." Her face fell and she looked grave. "You know, it wouldn't surprise me in the slightest if someone had used a curse against the poor man."

I nodded. "That's what it sounds like to me, too." However, it seemed unlikely we would ever know, I thought. "Hopefully, it will just be a one off." I glanced out of the window and noticed that the light had changed. "Oh no," I said. "Did they forecast showers today?"

"It's hot enough for a storm, certainly," Millicent said, fanning herself.

I waved Gloria over and asked for the bill. "Sorry Millicent, I need to get back to the inn. I've left the windows open upstairs. I wasn't expecting rain."

"Oh that's no problem, my dear girl," Millicent exclaimed, "let's do it again soon." I dropped ten pounds on the saucer Gloria had provided to settle the whole bill, gave Millicent a quick hug and made my way outside, where the air hung hot and sticky. Thundery showers seemed increasingly likely.

Dashing across the road to the village shop, I greeted Rhona, and quickly grabbed eggs, mushrooms, red cabbage, red onions and the local newspaper, intending to race up the road to the inn. However, while Rhona rang up my purchases I flipped through the paper to the article on the death at Whittle Inn on page five.

The artist's impression gave me little clue as to who he was. A sharp faced man in his mid-fifties, with a receding hairline, making him look rather like a monk. What hair he had left, was dark but speckled with grey, and about two inches long circling his bald crown. He had a gap between his two front teeth. Not an attractive man.

I scanned the article. There was very little in it—the police were obviously relying on the description and the image for potential leads into the man's identity.

Paying Rhona, I started home, waving at Millicent once more in the window of the cafe, and walking quickly up the hill, past the row of cottages, heading out of the village to the inn.

It was then that I replayed the conversation I'd had with the older woman over tea. Why had she assumed the man had been cursed? The article hadn't mentioned a cause of death at all, and it wasn't widespread knowledge. Why would Millicent have assumed a curse rather than a hundred other ways he could have met his end?

Was Millicent all she seemed? The thought had me shivering in surprise, and when the first enormous raindrops began falling, I took to my heels and ran as fast as I could towards the safety of the inn.

Out of breath by the time I reached the lane leading to Whittle Inn, I paused near the rusty gate and took shelter under a large oak tree. Placing my bags on the ground I leant against the trunk. I caught my breath, doubled over, while listening to the comforting pitter-patter of raindrops hitting the large green leaves above my head. It was a typically quiet weekday afternoon, with little traffic on the road, so I didn't have to worry about being seen, or looking stupid.

Eventually I straightened up, and to my surprise I heard a gentle hooing. I peered up into the oak tree but couldn't see Mr Hoo. It seemed far too early for him to be out and about anyway. Dusk was still hours away. Deciding I must be hearing things I bent down to pick up my bags. From somewhere behind me came the crack of a branch. I spun around. Leaving my bags where they were, I moved out of the shelter of the tree, scanning the area behind me, peering through the foliage there.

Rain beat loudly against the canopy of leaves. I held my breath, straining to hear anything else.

A faint crackling noise originating from somewhere near the inn drifted my way. I frowned. Someone was out here, close by, maybe just in front of me, perhaps only a few feet away, hiding among the trees, watching me as I waited and listened for them, but the crackling noise worried me. I turned my head, looking towards the inn, unsure what to do.

The rain eased slightly, and the breeze brought a hint of damp wood smoke. Someone, somewhere was having a bonfire.

Except it was the wrong time of year for a bonfire, and too early in the day for a barbeque. In any case the only property in the vicinity was the inn. Cold dread flooded through my veins, and everything else was forgotten. Leaving my bags, I ran hard up the lane, one hundred yards, two hundred and three. The crackling sound grew louder, and I cried out in fear.

"Please," I begged aloud, "not the inn. Not my inn."

Rounding the final bend in the trees so that the inn lay in front of me, my gaze darted wildly around, seeking trouble. The scent of smoke was stronger, and the sound of flames louder, but nothing looked amiss. The door was locked, the windows intact. I couldn't see a fire.

I ran around the side of the inn, towards the back, and at last I found the source of both the noise and the smell of smoke. The stable block was on fire. Orange flames licked at the side of the building, poking their hot tongues of fierce hatred through broken windows. I considered grabbing a fire extinguisher from the inn, but even twenty feet from the flames I understood it was much too late for a fire extinguisher. Nothing would calm this beast. At all.

I took to my heels once more, back down the lane, my legs pumping faster and faster, until I skidded heavily to a stop in front of the oak. I rummaged around in my hand bag for my mobile, but I couldn't find it. Practically in tears now, frustrated and angry with myself, I tipped the bag upside down and dumped keys, tissues, letters, lip balms, sweets and miscellaneous crap all over the ground. Sifting quickly through all of my rubbish yielded no phone. I must have left it in the tea shop.

I ran shaky hands through my hair. Nothing for it but to run back down to the village. Why hadn't I had a phone line installed at the inn yet? What a ridiculous oversight. I turned for the road and the village just as a sleek black car shot out of the next turning and zoomed off towards the village. I yelled and ran into the road after it, but it didn't stop. Fortunately, a car driving up behind me had to swerve to narrowly avoid me. It screeched to a halt.

I recognised the woman in her dark green mini. "Sally!" I cried. "Thank goodness. Can you help me? The inn's on fire! Do you have a phone I can borrow?"

CHAPTER FIFTEEN

It took the fire brigade several hours to dampen the fire down and extinguish it completely. I surveyed the smoking ruins of the stable block with dismay. There would be no renovating this and turning it into a luxury villa for more discerning guests. The site would have to be completely cleared.

More expense at a time when I could ill afford it.

Detective Gilchrist arrived on the scene at about the same time as Jed. The storm had passed and the sun was out. I squinted as I watched them walk up the lane together. Jed gave me a hug and I had to fight back the tears I wanted to shed in the face of his compassion. I didn't want Gilchrist to see me feeling weak.

Gilchrist spoke at some length with the lead fire-fighter, before heading my way to take a statement.

"It's a rum business this, isn't it?" Gilchrist said gravely. "Were you near when the fire broke out?"

"No. I was down in the village having tea," I said. "I fancied a treat, otherwise I would have been here. I could have stopped this."

"Perhaps it's better that you weren't," said Jed.

"Maybe it was an accident," I said. "Loose wires or something?"

"Definitely not an accident," Gilchrist confirmed. "The investigating fire officer says an accelerant was used, and they found a petrol can in the hedge behind the stable."

"Kids then?" I said hopefully, but Gilchrist led me back towards the inn. He pointed at some dark puddles on the ground.

"Notice anything?" he said, and squatted next to the puddle, agitating the water with his finger. I watched as swirls of colour danced greasily around each other, purple and green and blue. "Somebody was trying to burn the inn down, Ms Daemonne."

"Oh," I said as fear lodged like a stone in my throat, leaving me mute with horror. I remembered Lyle, the landlord at The Hay Loft. What had he said? "That place is a death trap. It wouldn't surprise me if it burned to the ground." I'd considered it a throwaway comment. What sort of people was I dealing with here? I was at risk of losing everything.

"Do you have insurance?" Jed asked. I shook my head. I had nothing, except the inn and the estate and all the debts that went with it.

"You haven't received any more threats?" Gilchrist asked.

"No."

"Threats?" Jed repeated. "What threats?"

I looked up at the inn, at its solid and growing familiarity. I sensed it waiting for me to act, so I pulled myself together, took strength from its strength, found anger to replace the fear that might otherwise have immobilised me, and finally located the voice and emotion to go with it.

"No," I said, "no more threats." I turned to Jed. "Just a stupid little note designed to scare me. But it doesn't."

"Nonetheless, Ms Daemonne, I would urge you to reconsider staying here until we can discover what is going on, and apprehend the person or persons involved."

"This is my home, Detective," I said firmly. "There is nowhere else I will feel safe, so this is where I'm staying."

"I—" Gilchrist began to say and I glared at him. He backed off.

"Listen. I can stay with you," Jed said, and both Gilchrist and I looked at him with new interest.

"I mean, there's plenty of space, and ..." he shrugged. "It might be good to have a man about the place." He looked doubtful, and I smiled.

"Do you have your own sleeping bag?" I asked.

Later, when the fire engines, officers and police had departed, and Jed had driven back into the village to collect some belongings, I carefully walked the perimeter of the inn, repeating the mantra of the previous evening; *Guard this space from all ill will and all those who wish us harm.* There was no doubt in my mind that the spell I had weaved to ward off negativity and bad feeling had saved the inn from a dismal end.

Yes, it was a blow to lose the stable block with its extra rooms, but at the end of the day this was a problem that was surmountable. Losing the inn would not have been so easy to shake off, under any circumstances.

I was thankful the spell had worked, given my

rustiness as a practitioner, now I needed to reinforce the magick and guard the inn. This would be vitally important if I decided to head up to London and leave the inn in Jed's care.

Once I'd finished the circumnavigation of the perimeter, I walked across the drive so that I could gaze up at the whole of the front of the building. I admired the windows with their bottle glass, each small square pane individually crafted by hand. In my mind's eye I stroked the great wooden beams, black with age, caressed the peeling paint work, smoothed the tiles on the roof. And most of all, I embraced the wonky walls, and drew them into my heart.

I recognised that in order to preserve this aging example of archaeological quirkiness, I would need to draw on my own heritage, on the very part of my being I had denied for so long. I would have to step up and become the witch my mother had always wanted me to be. I would need to reach out to the Elders, to those who could assist in my quest, and I would have to unleash my innate powers and practice the skills I had long neglected. I could only hope that those hostile inhabitants of Whittlecombe village who thought they had me on the run, were ready.

Chapter Sixteen

Instead of being floored by the fire, I dug deep and unearthed a newfound positivity. Having Jed around certainly lifted my general mood, and I found working with him fun. I started to visualise a proper future for the inn and began to collect my thoughts in a notebook, sketching plans, writing down ideas, sticking photos of furniture and furnishings that I fancied in between the pages. I wanted to go for a light-and-easy-but-traditional look, iron bedsteads juxtaposed with white or cream bedding, refurbished oak furniture, wooden floors and plenty of rugs, flowers and pictures. And I wanted to restore the bar to its former glory, with a dazzling array of colourful optics in front of mirrors polished to perfection, gleaming in the firelight.

"Look at this drawing," I instructed Jed over breakfast a few days after the fire, handing him my well-thumbed notebook. "We could create a check-in area, over in the corner, near the main door and next to the stairs."

"Can't your guests just check in at the bar?" Jed asked, spooning muesli into his mouth and chewing hard. "That's what they do at The Hay Loft."

"I know," I sniffed, "and that doesn't seem very welcoming to me," I said. "I want the people who stay here to feel that Whittle Inn is a little more distinguished."

"More upmarket you mean?"

"I don't know about upmarket. Just different to that. I worked for a while in the bar of a boutique hotel near Regents Park. It only had twelve bedrooms, and they were tiny. But each bedroom was different to the other, and guests could choose which style they preferred. I liked that. We could theme the rooms."

"Like a blue room and a green room?"

I sighed and smiled wryly. Men. "You could think of it that way, yes. I was thinking more of naming them after film stars or writers."

"Okay. A JK Rowling and a Stephen King room? Good idea. Frighten the clientele away."

I laughed. "Well yes, I need to work out exactly the kind of customer I'm trying to attract and that will help me decide on a theme. I don't want to enter into bitter rivalry with the Hay Loft particularly. I don't think that will do either of us any good."

"So whom then?"

"I have a few ideas," I said, chewing on the lid of my biro. "These are all decisions I need to take before we start on painting and decorating, of course."

"Have you decided what you want to do in here?" Jed asked, gesturing around at the large L shaped bar area.

"Yes, I have. Come with me." I jumped up and grabbed Jed's arm. He resisted at first as he hadn't finished his breakfast, but I tsk-tsk'd at him and he followed me to the back of the old store room.

"I'd like some Georgian doors or similar to open out here," I said, and then dragged him back through the bar, down the corridor, through the kitchen and out of the back door. "It's important to me that we have a nice seating area where the guests can enjoy the garden. I want to have this entire area landscaped. It's a perfect place to look out at the woods and just chill out."

He nodded. "What about the stable?"

We both studied the area, me with great sadness. "For now, we're going to have to clear the site completely, so that it's not an eye-sore when people come out here. At least we'll have a wonderful view."

I stopped.

Behind where the stables had once stood, the tree line was thinner. A number of older trees had burned with the stable, and beyond those, younger, thinner trees stretched back for about eight feet. The gaps allowed me to see the field beyond. Farm land, that hadn't been tended in many a year.

I didn't own that land.

I could clearly see people in the field. Two men, walking towards the edge of my boundary.

"Who are they?" I asked Jed, directing his attention to the men, both clad in wellington boots and flat plaid caps. He shook his head and I followed his lead as he ducked and crept towards the line of trees.

We carefully made our way through the sparse foliage and hid ourselves low to the ground. I nestled among the ferns and undergrowth, pressing my face against one side of a fallen tree trunk. The smell of damp earth and the lingering scent of smoke tickled my nose, while small insects buzzed around my face. I brushed them away and listened as the voices came closer.

"We can build as far as here for now, give or take a few metres," a familiar voice was saying. I peered carefully over the edge of the tree trunk, but the men were turned away from me. "This meadow land stretches down to the road, and then back this way you have a couple of hectares of forest area you could utilise."

"What if we misjudge?"

"Misjudge the boundaries? And go further, you mean?"

"Let's say, we colour outside the lines?"

The first voice harrumphed his amusement. "That's difficult to say. There's every chance the planning department could insist you pulled down any houses you built."

"If somebody complained you mean?" The second voice demanded.

"Well, yes ..."

"But we might be able to apply for retroactive planning?"

"That's a possibility. I wouldn't stake my life on it."

"You don't have to stake your life, Pimm. Surely the council will be more than pleased to see Whittle Inn bulldozed."

My mouth fell open in shock and I looked across at Jed, wide-eyed and furious.

Charles Pimm. My surveyor.

"You could be right, Gladstone. It's been an eyesore for years."

Gladstone Talbot-Lloyd. I might have known. I had the urge to jump out of my hiding place and shout them down, intent on giving them a piece of my mind, but Jed leaned across to place a placating hand on my thigh. He shook his head slowly and mouthed the word, 'no.'

"I think we should go ahead. It has to be worth the risk. She's one woman, alone, and a stranger in town. We can act fast and make sure we have no complaints from anyone locally. None that anyone will listen to anyway. We can neutralise them if we have to. Let's loosen the purse strings."

"I'll need more capital," Pimm replied silkily.

"You'll get it. Talk to our contact," Talbot-Lloyd growled.

"And the complainants in the village? I'm not sure how we can keep them all quiet. Many of them will object to a larger housing estate being built on this land."

"Nimbys. They want more housing but don't want to sacrifice a field to build it on. Ignore them. Everyone else does."

"But what about Whittle Inn and the Daemonne woman?"

"Don't worry. I have a team working on it."

Stealthily, we followed the pair as they made their way back to their vehicles. Neither of them drove a sleek black car, like the one I'd seen leaving the field, the day of the fire. Talbot-Lloyd owned a mud-spattered and fly encrusted navy Range Rover, while Pimm was driving a shiny silvery gold BMW. I watched them disappear down the road, a bitter taste coating the back of my throat.

Jed caught my hand, sensing my distress, and pulled me back towards the inn. "Come on," he said. "I'll make some tea and we can think about what to do next."

We perched opposite each other, at the bar, nursing our mugs. I felt cold inside and out, but oddly calm. What's that old adage? Know thine enemy? Well now I did.

Except thinking about it, I didn't really, did I?

I stared into space, trying to weigh up what I knew. Yes, either of those men might have been responsible for the fire, but given that neither of them were of the craft, they couldn't have used the Curse of Madb on the body I'd found outside.

"What are you thinking?" Jed asked gently and I brought my focus back to him.

"I'm so confused."

"You ought to speak to Gilchrist. Tell him what you overheard."

"Do you think he'll believe us?" I asked. "What evidence do we have? Surely it's all hearsay."

Jed shrugged.

I placed my mug on the bar, and drew a large square in my notebook. "It's almost like we have two separate problems." I sketched in the inn, and then drew the boundary to the right hand side. "On the one hand we have a property developer building here," I indicated the field next to us, "who wants to get his filthy paws on the inn and the land, so that he can develop here ..." I shaded my land, "And on the other, there is some dark magic afoot. But I can't see how the two are linked. Talbot Lloyd and Pimm, as wicked and evil as the pair of them are, are in no way, shape or form, part of my kind."

"You'd know for sure?" Jed asked.

"I'm certain I would."

I would, wouldn't I?

"So what's the connection?" Jed asked, watching me carefully.

"Maybe there isn't one? Maybe I'm just unlucky

enough to have enemies at every turn." I sighed. "But I can't rule anything out. If we only knew the identity of the man who was killed out the back here, then that might help me discover who killed him."

"Perhaps you're wrong and it wasn't a curse? Perhaps he did fall."

"While scaling the outside wall? There had been no break-in, remember," I reminded Jed. "The inn was secure." I turned my thoughts back to the discovery of the body and the distinctive ruby ring.

Jed stared at my diagram. "I could go to the planning office at the local council offices, and examine planning applications for the housing development next door. See how far it stretches, and ask about grounds to appeal, if you like?"

"That would be helpful." I jumped from my stool.

"What are you going to do?"

"I'm going to London. There's some people I need to reacquaint myself with."

Chapter Seventeen

Luca Shadowmender resided in a small house on a modern housing estate in Surbiton. From outside you would never have known that he was one of the most powerful, renowned and experienced wizards in Europe. Originating from Poland, he had crossed the channel as a boy with his parents. Now in his late seventies or early eighties, there was little about magick he didn't know or couldn't find out for you. Respected worldwide for his wisdom, his compassion and his great learning, he had been head of my mother's coven all my life, and therefore in many ways he was my spiritual leader too.

I had of course forsaken my calling half a lifetime ago, and now I wasn't sure how warmly I would be received. Nonetheless, I had to try.

As I walked up his gravel driveway, I spotted him pottering in his cluttered garage. The doors had been pulled wide open, displaying shelves crammed with neatly labelled plastic boxes of metal, rubber, glass, and wired components, and myriad other random items. He appeared to be tinkering with a child's tricycle.

When he noticed me hovering outside, he lay his tools down and walked towards me with an uneven gait. Hunched over, his gnarled fingers gripped a hand-carved walking stick.

"Alfhild," he greeted me in his sing-song fashion. "I left the kettle singing on the stove. Come. Come."

Of course he would have been aware I was visiting even though I had arrived unannounced.

I followed him as he slowly manoeuvred around the side of the garage to his back garden, beautifully laid out in its summer splendour, a mix of herbs and flowers, fruits and vegetables. Shadowmender was obviously a green fingered wizard, and this was a suburban paradise. I climbed up a step into his kitchen. As soon as the back door had been closed behind us, he straightened up, flexed his hands, then threw his walking stick towards the hall. It twirled in the air, flew the four or five yards, and landed perfectly in place on the umbrella stand.

"You aren't surprised to see me," I said and his watery blue eyes sparkled with mischief.

"Of course not. All things are foretold if you know what to look for."

He indicated a door to the right. "Come through, come through," he said and almost skipped into his lounge. I remembered visiting this house with my mother soon after my father's disappearance. From the outside it was very much a bog standard 1970s semi-detached, complete with double glazing and pebbledash finish. But once inside, you were transported into some late-eighteenth, early-nineteenth century alchemist's hideaway. In the kitchen Shadowmender had a huge range, complete with cauldron, while in the living room, the walls were lined with oak shelving. Leather bound books with gilt lettering were piled high on every available surface. Odd gadgets, clocks, stuffed animals - and plenty of live ones too - completed the look. A fire burned in a Victorian grate, and yet the house did not have a chimney. It was quite extraordinary.

Shadowmender pointed at a large over-stuffed chair, covered in midnight blue velvet. I shooed a sleeping tabby cat away so I could sit, fortunately not overly precious about cat hair on my dress. It would brush off.

"How are you, Alf?" Shadowmender sank into his own chair with a sigh of relief.

I knew he was referring to the death of my mother. "I'm okay," I replied. "I've been keeping busy." Guiltily I realised I hadn't been thinking of my mother overly much. We hadn't been close and I hadn't seen a great deal of her, so her loss hadn't made any great impact

"With Whittle Inn?" the Wizard smiled. "Ah." Of course he would know about that too.

"Yes. It needs a lot of work."

"And you need a huge amount of patience, no doubt. Although, I'm sure you'll make a wonderful success of it, when the time comes."

"I do hope so."

We regarded each other for a moment, and I fidgeted in the chair.

"What brings you here, Alf?" Shadowmender asked eventually.

I blew the air out of my lungs. Where to start? I jumped in, my words faltering. "I want to pick up on my training. I'm having a few issues with people who seem to want to either scare me away from the inn, or force me into selling it, or even, I fear, who are seeking to destroy it. I want to be able to protect myself, and the inn, and Jed ... my friend."

"Hmm." Shadowmender regarded me thoughtfully before standing, and walking towards me, no trace of stiffness or disability. He took my head gently between his hands, tipping my face up and staring into my eyes. I watched his pupils widen. He stayed that way for some time, reaching deep inside me, delicately probing my head and my heart with his unbroken stare. Finally, he blinked and pulled his gaze away, without letting his hands drop.

He increased the pressure on the sides of my skull. A sharp pain stabbed until he withdrew his hands slowly, pulling something out of my thoughts. His hands widened and the pain lessened until it disappeared completely. He brought his hands slowly together as though to clap. I caught a brief glimpse of something slick and black pulsing on his hand, the size of a small pebble, and then he crushed it between his hands. There was a small explosion of dust and a spitting sound and he shook his empty hands at the fire, and rubbed them on his gown.

"You don't need that," he said gently, and I wondered what it had been.

Next Shadowmender picked up a clear glass orb from the table next to him and held it up between us. It caught the light from the fire, and glittered in his hand. He turned it this way and that, studying what he could see within. I leaned in a little closer and spotted shadows racing across the surface of the glass, but nothing that I could read. He muttered something I couldn't make out and twisted the orb sharply, then handed it to me. It was surprisingly heavy. I turned it as I'd seen Shadowmender do, and looked deep into the heart of the glass.

"What do you see?" he asked.

"I see the inn!" I said excitedly.

"Good. Yes. How is it?"

"It looks fine. Oh!" I laughed in delight as a tiny Jed walked across the middle of the orb from the inn to his van. It was like watching camera footage on my mobile. "There's Jed. I wonder what he's doing?" I watched him get in his van and drive off.

"The inn is fine. Your friend is fine. You did a good job of warding negativity away from the inn."

I shook my head. "I should have walked the whole perimeter – all of my boundaries. My carelessness cost me the stable block."

"Perhaps," Shadowmender acquiesced, and resumed his seat, "but given how long it's been since you last practised magick of this kind, I'd say you did a very good job."

"Thank you."

"I'm sure you feel a little rusty, but trust me, everything you will need to see you through this trying time, all the skills and the powers and the strength, you have those within you. Call them out when you need them. Keep working on your skills."

Shadowmender nodded. "Yes. Let magick into every aspect of your life. But honestly? You've probably been doing that all along, even if you were in denial about who you are and what you're capable of."

He was right of course.

"You were an excellent student. Your skills will flood back when you allow them to."

"So no more training?"

"You can practise on your own. You'll make mistakes of course, but that's how we all learn, Alf. How we become stronger and wiser." He shifted in his seat. "But don't be afraid to seek help from the Elders, or from our coven. We will always be with you one way or another. Just as your ancestors are."

His words had great wisdom. If I allowed my thoughts and senses to run free and easy, if I allowed my being to stray beyond restricted boundaries, if I allowed myself to be open to all there was, I would be a better witch. Compassion, kindness, empathy sensitivity, strength and love. Those were the gifts bestowed upon me to make use of as I deemed fit.

"If there are gaps in your knowledge, and of course there are bound to be, make use of the library in Wisdom House. Your membership has never lapsed, you know."

Of course, Wisdom House on Celestial Street. Many an hour I'd spent in there, scrunched over an ancient and scarred desk, carved with the initials of hundreds of scholars before me, hidden among the centuries old shelving. It had been a favourite hangout of mine, even after my father had gone. It provided an escape from the world, and far from simply stocking tomes of historical magic and folk lore, it had quite often had the latest comics and magazines of a purely secular nature. I suppose the thinking was, how else would some traditional and dyed-in-the-wool magickal folk comprehend the world they found themselves living in without the tools to instruct them? Hooray for *Cosmopolitan* and *Country Life* magazines.

"You're right," I said. "I should take the craft more seriously. Thank you for the pointers."

"That's what I'm here for. To help you grow and learn. We all need to keep doing so, no matter how old and decrepit we get." He laughed and his wizened face lit up with amusement.

"There's something else I wanted to talk to you about," I said, and I burrowed around in my bag for my notebook, handing it over to Shadowmender, open at the page I wanted him to study.

He glanced at my drawing, his brow furrowed. "Where have you seen this?" he asked. In among all the drawings and plans I had made for the inn, I had created a rough sketch of the ring I'd seen on the body outside the inn, and coloured it the best I could – red and gold - but not quite recreating the spectacular shimmer of the gold shooting through the ruby.

"It was on the body I found outside the inn the afternoon I arrived." Shadowmender nodded his understanding. He'd obviously heard of the incident.

"What happened to the ring, do you know?"

"I assume the police have it. It was still on his body when they took him away."

"That's a shame." Shadowmender stroked his beard thoughtfully. "Have you heard of the Circle of Querkus?"

"No."

"They are a secretive all-male band of warlocks, witches and druids. Not to be messed with. They are ancient protectors of forests and woodlands. Membership is top secret. On the whole their intentions are good, but their methods are shadowy to say the least. Over the past century or so, there have been rumours that certain factions within the Circle have gone rogue."

I was puzzled. "Meaning what?"

"Certain members have broken away and formed a group known as The Mori. Their heads have been turned. It's the usual story. Money, power. Instead of providing protection for the great woodland spaces across the world, they are desperate to see off their brothers, the Circle of Querkus, and have free rein of the land left behind. They can only do that by destroying every hectare of forest they can lay their hands to, because when there are no woodlands there will be no need for the powerful Circle of Querkus. To that end they are in league with mere mortals, an uneasy and unnatural alliance for temporary and gutless glory." Shadow-mender held my gaze. "I can't reiterate strongly enough that The Mori should not be trifled with. Rumours abound of corruption at the highest levels, of blackmail, treachery, murder. That ring – in green – would be recognisable as something the Circle of Querkus would wear. The red tells us it is The Mori."

"The murder victim was a member of The Mori?"

"It would appear so."

I was more confused than ever. "So what do they want with the inn?"

"I would assume it is not Whittle Inn that is of interest to them."

His words drew me up short. How stupid of me. "No, of course it isn't," I clapped a hand to my head in alarm. "The inn and the grounds are incidental. But it sits in the estate that I inherited, a great portion of which is entirely woodland, and is part of a much larger forest area around Whittlecombe. Speckled Wood is the thin end of the wedge."

"There you have it," Shadowmender said calmly enough, but his face was troubled.

"How do I ward off an army of The Mori, intent on destroying my trees?" I asked in horror.

"Not an army," Shadowmender insisted forcefully. "Don't worry on that score. But they do box clever. They will have a team of mortals helping them, because that's the way the world works in the twenty-first century. They need the bureaucrats and the local politicians. They need administrators and bankers. You mustn't trust anyone."

Aghast, I thought of the villagers back in Whittlecombe, of Rhona and Stan, Millicent and Jed, Talbot-Lloyd and everyone else I had met over the weeks, and the sudden sense of isolation completely took the wind out of my sails. "Oh," I said. "I've been so naïve." My knees quivered and I was glad to be seated.

Shadowmender reached over and patted my hand. "It is fortuitous indeed that you found your way here today. I will send people to you. Together they can cast a wider circle of protection around the inn and Speckled Wood." He smiled wryly. "And you won't feel so alone."

Tears pricked at my eyelids. He understood then. "Thank you," I whispered.

"You'll also need to fight back against those who might use 'legal' means to rob you of what is rightfully yours." He emphasised the word legal. "These constructs that humankind creates. Watch out for them. Compulsory purchase. Town planning and the like. The Mori will have friends in high places, you'll need to keep a careful eye out. Who is your lawyer?"

"Penelope Quigwell."

"Ah, excellent. Tell her all. She will help you."

"Alright," I said. I was heading to her chambers anyway. "There's this you should look at too," I said, reaching into my bag once more for the newspaper report and the police artist's impression of the victim. "This is the man who died. Do you recognise him?"

I handed the paper over, and Shadowmender

studied the article with interest, but shook his head. "This is the one who was wearing the ring? He is not someone I've come across." I felt disappointed. Knowing who he was might help me figure out whom he was working for. "The Mori do not like to spend time in the spotlight. They inherited that from their brothers in the Circle of Querkus. Their members are not well known. That's the way they prefer it. But there is a wizard in your neck of the woods who may well recognise this chap if he is a local. I'll put you in touch with him. His name is Mr Kephisto and he runs The Story Keeper, a bookshop in Abbotts Cromleigh, not many miles from Whittle Inn if I recall."

I watched as he smoothed the newspaper out, burning the image onto his retina. "You know, there is an interesting twist to this that we haven't considered, Alf."

"What's that?" I stared down at the image too.

"Someone out there is on your side. They did you a favour by killing this chap."

His words came like a bolt from the blue. I hadn't considered that. Whomever had killed a member of The Mori had done so on purpose, knowing exactly what they were doing.

"My goodness, yes! I heard the post-mortem

results. I think the perpetrator used the Curse of Madb. Fractured bones, but no other trauma."

The wizard lifted his eyebrows. "Powerful magic indeed. So there is another witch or a wizard in your vicinity. Perhaps one who has made themselves known to you, or perhaps not. I urge you to speak to Kephisto. Perhaps he can help you. What we don't want is a war breaking out in Devon."

I stood to take my leave and Shadowmender followed me to the door, summoning his walking stick from its place in the rack. As we stepped outside into his beautiful garden, he hunched over once more.

"Mind how you go, Alf. And keep me posted. I'll send help as soon as possible."

Forewarned is forearmed, they say, and by the time I arrived at Celestial Street, I have to admit to feeling more grounded and less fearful. For sure, by the sound of it at least, I had a group of dangerous warlocks on my doorstep, and to be fair they were probably in league with Talbot-Lloyd and intent on trying to find a way to extract my land from me, but now I knew I had people on my side too. Shadow-mender had promised to send others to help me, and it appeared I had at least one ally on the ground in Whittlecombe.

I wondered who that might be.

Millicent seemed the obvious answer, although I didn't have her pegged as a member of a top secret organisation such as the Circle of Querkus. But perhaps it was a double bluff and she was being secretive while totally out there.

The complexity of it all was enough to make my head spin.

At The Half Moon Inn, I paused, wondering whether to check in for the night. The intention was to pay Penelope Quigwell an unexpected visit. If she refused to see me then and there, I would camp out until she did. I needed answers. I wanted to know where the missing money from my inheritance had disappeared to. The fact that Wizard Shadow-mender had rated her so highly gave me pause, for I had been starting to seriously doubt her loyalty to her clients, and pondering on whether she had been double-crossing me. Well, time would tell. If I couldn't see her today, I would stay overnight at The Half Moon and try and catch her in the morning if all else failed.

I wandered up to the clock shop, my overnight bag on my shoulder, pondering a strategy for the next few hours. Staring absently in through the window, I was surprised to spot Charles Pimm, my surveyor making a purchase at the till. Dressed in a smart suit, his hair slicked smoothly across his forehead, he looked quite different to the man I'd seen in the field next to the inn a few days ago. What was he doing in Celestial Street?

He stepped lively, heading out of the shop towards me. I made myself as small as possible, and shrunk into the window, holding my breath as he passed by me and praying he wouldn't notice me. He didn't.

He skirted me and marched towards the door to my left, 14b. I listened as he pressed the buzzer and announced himself. The door opened and he made his way in. I followed him, and reached the door in the final millisecond before it sprang closed, and paused there with my hand holding it ajar slightly, allowing Pimm time to climb the stairs. Then when I was hopeful he was out of sight, I quietly pushed the door wide and let myself in, creeping up the stairs after him.

I waited near the top, just where the stairs curved around. If I climbed any higher I would be seen and that would give the game away rather.

As luck would have it, Quigwell's crotchety assistant wasn't at his desk, so Quigwell herself came out of her office to meet Pimm.

"Do you have what I need?" he asked, his tone haughty, arrogant in the extreme.

"No-one can supply what you need," Quigwell replied, her own voice icy.

"You need to try harder," Pimm said. "We have an agreement."

"Take this," Quigwell said, "and leave. I don't want anybody to see you here." I looked back down the stairs in alarm. Was he going to leave already? And what had she just given him? I tentatively took a step backwards.

"We don't need your money, woman. Get us the deeds to that land," Pimm growled.

"It won't be long now, I'm sure. She'll be bankrupt by the end of the month and we can foreclose. I can wrap it all up very quickly."

Were they talking about me and my inn? Cold fury coursed through me. Part of me wanted to march up the stairs and confront them there and then, but something stayed my hand. What would they do if they were aware of how much I knew about them and their plans?

Cautiously I crept backwards, inching down the stairs.

"Make sure you're ready to make a move straight away when I tell you," Pimm ordered and Quigwell murmured something I couldn't catch. They were saying their goodbyes. I moved quicker, the stairs creaking, and yanked the door open, then dashed into the street looking for somewhere to hide, certain they had heard me. It had to be the clock shop. I ran inside and melted carefully into the shadows between a pair of grandfather clocks. Holding my breath, I watched from my vantage point as Pimm dashed from 14b and peered up and down the street, then he turned to look inside the clock shop. He stared straight at me and my heart stopped. He had to see me, and yet he didn't react. Then as all the clocks struck four, and a cacophony of noise erupted from the shop, he grimaced and turned about, marching down the street in the direction of the bookshop. I crept out of my hiding place and watched him go, saw his uneasy glances, left and right, before he disappeared.

Breathing a sigh of relief, I looked around. The proprietor of the clock shop had seen everything and studied me through knowing eyes. I considered him, questioning his intentions, waiting to see if he would challenge me, but he offered a slight smile, and bowed.

Feeling wary, I snuck out of the clock shop, looking around me and up at the windows of the offices above the shops. Of Quigwell there was no sign. Was Shadowmender wrong about her? I wasn't sure she could be trusted at all.

Relieved to get away, I stuck to the shadows and

cautiously made my way down the alley to the bookshop.

Time to head back to Devon to ward off further problems.

CHAPTER NINETEEN

By the time I arrived at The Story Keeper in Abbotts Cromleigh, it was nearly ten in the evening. With no train station in Abbotts Cromleigh, I'd had to endure a painfully long bus journey from Exeter, although the roads were relatively clear at that time of night. Perhaps I should have headed straight for the inn, but my sixth sense was telling me to make hay while the sun shone. Not that the sun was shining, you understand. A large milky moon was climbing in the sky, and the stars were bright overhead. The lights in the bookshop were out, but a glow emanated from the flat above.

The Storykeeper was housed in a building of a similar age to Whittle Inn. Its front bowed out over the narrow road, like the prow of an Elizabethan ship. Unlike the inn, the shop was beautifully kept.

The paintwork gleamed brightly white even in the relative gloom of the evening.

I hovered in front of the door, unsure how to proceed, until I heard a click and the door swung inwards, away from me. Cautiously, I climbed a few steps and moved into the shop. The smell of new books tickled my nose and the door gently closed behind me, the lock clicking back into place. I didn't feel concerned. The shop had an air of calm.

I followed the light, climbing a horribly rickety staircase, rather sponge-like, to the mezzanine level.

A large black crow, balanced comfortably on a perch, watched my progress with interest. "Kephisto," it called, its black eyes glittering with intelligence. "Kephisto."

I jumped, startled when an old man sitting in a large armchair next to the bookshelves called, "I hear you, Caius, pipe down." I hadn't spotted him there.

"Hi," I said.

"Greetings traveller," Kephisto replied and stood to shake my hand. "You're Alfhild, I take it? You've had a long day. I'm Kephisto. Shadowmender informed me you'd be coming."

"Alf." I said. "You can call me Alf. I'm sorry it's so late."

"That's not a problem. Time is relative. You must

be weary. I've made us some tea." He gestured towards a small table laden with a teapot, cups and saucers and a plate of sandwiches and mini-quiches. My favourites.

"Thank you," I said, grateful for the thought. I'd had such a mad dash panic through London to catch my train that I hadn't stopped anywhere to pick up a snack, and then the train to Exeter contained no buffet car. It had been a fraught journey. I'd made myself very small in my seat, worrying the whole time that Pimm would be on board somewhere too, and would work his way through the carriages at any minute and spot me.

I slouched into the chair Kephisto indicated, weary to my bones, thinking I could easily fall asleep right there, but helped myself to a tuna fish sandwich and watched as Kephisto poured tea. The amber liquid glowed in the soft light from numerous lamps dotted around the place, and just one mouthful seemed to ease the tension from my shoulders and help me relax.

"What is this?" I asked, sipping at the brew once more.

"Oh you know, lavender, chamomile, a few other pinches of herbs," Kephisto said.

"Should I be worried?" I speculated out loud.

"It's beginning to be difficult to know the difference between my enemies and my friends."

Kephisto laughed cheerfully. "Well my dear, that depends a great deal on what it is that you want from your future. You came to see me."

"Wizard Shadowmender recommended I do that, because you know who's who, down here in the West Country."

"That's true for the most part, I certainly do. Are you looking for someone in particular? Do you have a name?"

"No name," I said, and placed my cup and saucer on the table in front of me, reaching for my bag. "Just an image. An illustration created by an artist." I handed the newspaper over to Kephisto who turned it to the light and examined it in minute detail. "I found this man dead out the back of Whittle Inn when I arrived there a few weeks ago. At first I thought he had been trying to break in, or that he had been killed and left there by someone who was trying to ruin me. I wasn't overly concerned."

Kephisto peered over the top of his spectacles at me. "So what changed your mind?"

I didn't immediately answer, I wanted to see what Mr Kephisto had to say about the person in the image. Kephisto offered a wry smile and looked once more at the photo.

"Well it's been a few years but I'd say this is Edvard Zadzinsky. His forefathers came from Eastern Europe, and it is widely thought they were all member of the Circle of Querkus. Powerful warlocks."

"Shadowmender told me about the Circle of Querkus, but he didn't know this ... Edward."

"Edvard. I'm surprised word didn't reach Shadowmender about this man. Even as a child he was a bad'n. Right from the word go. I knew him as a pup. An unusually gifted liar, and master manipulator. Found it easy to pit his siblings and friends off against each other. He had no honour. Never a good word to say about anyone. Would never take responsibility for anything he did, or any problems he caused. I always felt uncomfortable in his presence. He disappeared from my radar about forty years ago, and apart from occasional sightings of him, I don't know what he's been up to." Kephisto removed his spectacles, pulled a cloth from his pocket and proceeded to clean them. I could see him thinking and remained quiet.

Finally, he replaced the spectacles on the bridge

of his nose and looked at me. "You found him dead, you say?"

"Yes. And the post mortem found fractures to all his major bones, but no other trauma."

"The Curse of Madb," Kephisto muttered in a low voice.

I nodded. "Wizard Shadowmender said he is likely to be a member of The Mori?"

"Sadly that's very probable," Kephisto replied. "It's a worry."

"But more importantly, at the moment at least, I need to know who this Edvard was working for. I need to understand exactly who my enemies are, and who I can trust if I ever want to get the inn renovated and back up and working. Just this afternoon I've found my lawyer is in cahoots with the surveyor I used when I took over the inn. It appears they're working together to try to take the inn and my land off me. But is there anyone else? Are they all in league with The Mori?"

"You're right to be suspicious, and you're also correct that there's a team at work. The Mori will work very closely with ordinary mortals to make gains and destroy the forests. Who do you know that stands to gain the most from the destruction of your land?" Kephisto asked.

"Gladstone Talbot-Lloyd I imagine. He's a landowner who is talking about building houses on the field next to mine. He'd love to expand."

"Gladstone Talbot-Lloyd. The name rings a bell. I'll check him out and let you know."

I nodded and yawned, quickly covering my mouth with my hand. "Sorry," I said. "I don't mean to be rude. I'm done in."

"You must stay here tonight," Kephisto said and when I shook my head, intending to get back to the inn at the earliest opportunity, he insisted. "Getting back to Whittlecombe at this time of night will not be straightforward. Far better that you rest now and go first thing. I have a chaise upstairs that you're most welcome to use, assuming you don't want to sleep in an armchair, that is."

He was right and I was too tired to argue. "I'll just let Jed know I'm not coming home," I said and tried to call him from my phone. When he didn't pick up I left a voicemail and texted him for good measure.

"All done?" asked Mr Kephisto with a smile, and I nodded.

I turned to follow the old wizard but my phone beeped twice. I glanced at the screen. A message from Jed. "Sorry, I missed you. Just having a swift pint at The Hay Loft! See you in the morning X."

That seemed fair enough. All work and no play would make Jed a dull boy, I supposed. Leaving my phone, jacket and bag where they were, I followed the Mr Kephisto upstairs. I was asleep before he had time to hand me a blanket.

A few hours later I was awake though, listening to the creaks and groans of a building I was unused to. I lay on the chaise, aware of how hard it was, my heart hammering in my chest as I tried to make sense of all that was happening. On the one hand, I appeared to have thrown my lot in with Wizard Shadowmender and his friends, including Kephisto, none of whom I knew well, and on the other I – or perhaps the inn – had drawn the attention of The Mori.

Someone had killed a member of The Mori, and as yet, I wasn't entirely sure that the killer was a friend or a foe, or even who they were. In addition to that, a number of mortals wanted my land, and fortuitously for them, The Mori were happy to help them.

A tangled web indeed.

For the most part I yearned to get back to the inn, but another small part of me wanted to take to my heels and run far away where no-one would ever find me. For now, sleep claimed me once again.

Abbotts Cromleigh and Whittlecombe were virtually neighbours in the grand scheme of things, separated only by a river without a bridge. This meant venturing almost the whole way back to Exeter on the bus and then swapping buses and doubling back on the other side of the river.

I figured a broomstick would make things easier.

Or I could learn to drive.

After a frustrating and slow journey, I was finally dropped in Whittlecombe much to my relief, and half walked, half-jogged my way out of the village and up the lane to my wonky inn. I slowed down as I approached the drive, and gazed up at my building with something approaching great fondness. Jed came out of the front door and I waved.

"Jed!"

He spotted me and beamed. "Thank goodness you're here. I was starting to get worried," he enveloped me in a hug. It felt good.

"Sorry I couldn't make it home last night," I said, enjoying the close contact with him. "I did say that might be a possibility."

"It's not that. It's more that we have some unexpected visitors. I've tried to tell them the inn isn't habitable yet, but they're just not listening to me. They're insistent that they stay here."

"Visitors?" I asked frowning. "Perhaps they're the people that Shadowmender was sending to help us."

"Shadowmender? Help with what?"

"I have a lot to explain to you, Jed."

A figure appeared at the door clad in a bright red suit with a yellow Hawaiian shirt and matching yellow winkle pickers. He had dyed black hair, a la 1950s Elvis, and long sideburns.

"Hey, Jed," he drawled. "Would it be okay if we put a couple of chickens in the oven, only we're going to be building up an appetite you know?" He spotted me and nodded. "Hey, baby. Are you, Alfhild?"

"Alf, yes. And you are?"

"Mortimer Bowe at your service, honey. Dressed to impress and ready for action."

"Great!" I enthused. His choice of clothes was interesting to say the least.

"We received word from Shadowmender and we're happy to help, given we're virtually neighbours."

"You're from?"

"Lostwithiel."

Cornwall. Very nice. "It's good to have you here, Mortimer."

"Our pleasure." Turning to Jed he repeated, "About the chickens?"

"They're frozen." Jed pointed out.

"Not to worry, buddy. We have a spell that will take care of that." He dashed back inside and I could hear him calling someone else.

"When he says chickens ... Why not *a* chicken? How many guests do we have?"

"Around a dozen," Jed replied and my mouth dropped open.

"That many? How will we put them up?"

Jed made an exaggerated shrug. "I'm not the innkeeper. I just paint things," he said deadpan. I smacked his arm. "Ow."

"A dozen?" I asked again. I stood on the step and peered into the main room of the inn, observing an odd assortment of eccentric beings lounged on my mismatched chairs. One unfortunate had been forced to sit on the ladder.

I withdrew my head. “Are they all as original as Mortimer?”

“Oh, he’s the tip of the iceberg, believe me.”

“Interesting times,” I replied and braced myself for whatever came next.

It transpired that Wizard Shadowmender had provided me with a motley collection of souls, but all of them useful. Mortimer, and his partner Virginia, were hedge witches, charged with the care of the woodland around Restormel Castle and the River Fowey in the neighbouring county of Cornwall. They had buddied up with Red Daltry, an Earl of the realm and warlock currently residing in the New Forest, and Rhys Talog, a wizard hailing from the Gwydir Forest in Betws-y-Coed.

In addition to them, we welcomed a number of druids from Somerset - Rafe, Lois and Simon - and three witches from the Highlands - Bob, Tess and Andrew, and a weasel-faced witch who claimed ancestry from a leprechaun, whose name was

Finbarr. He seemed to have a lot in common with Jemima, which made them an unlikely pair as Jemima stood 6 ft. 6 inches in her stockinged feet. Originating from Brighton, Jemima had brought along Bryony who sported bright green dreadlocks, and Tiger, a young goth who looked an awful lot like the late Brandon Lee. Fourteen in total.

Over the course of the next few hours, I bustled around trying to organise sleeping arrangements, opening rooms that had been shut up for years, while Jed tried to arrange food to feed an army, which was pretty much what this brigands of odd bods amounted to.

I have to be honest. They seemed like a decent bunch, although not exactly helpful. Red was all for creating a bonfire in the middle of the reception room for example, until Jed patiently pointed out that a fireplace existed and simply needed sweeping so there was no need to create a crater in the middle of the floor. At that point Finbarr offered to conjure up a chimney sweep and before anybody could stop him he did so in the form of a number of pixies, each less than a foot high, who exploded from a pile of wood shavings on the ground and leapt into action, scurrying up the chimney. Accompanied by the sound of a million brush strokes, centuries worth of soot, pigeon bones and bird nests crashed to the floor, and the debris billowed out around us in a thick black cloud.

Jed's face was a picture as I held my hands to my head, aghast at the amount of mess. Virginia laughed at me.

"What's a little soot?" she asked. "We'll have a grand fire burning in that grate before you know it."

"So much to clean up," I said and gestured at the piles of rubble and dust, aware from experience just how quickly the mess would be tracked through the inn.

"So, conjure up your followers," Finbarr said helpfully in his sing-song Irish brogue.

"My followers?" I asked, looking about me, and hoping I wouldn't spot more of Finbarr's pixies.

"Did you ever see a witch with more followers than this one?" Finbarr asked the company and every one of them shook their heads.

"And I never saw this many followers in one place who were so intent on being helpful," said Rhys. "I certainly wish mine were."

"What sort of followers?" I asked.

"Ghosts," said Tiger gravely, his black eyes

following something behind me. "Dozens of them. Summon them and they will come."

"Ghosts?" I glanced behind my shoulder to see what Tiger was looking at, and as if for the first time I became aware of the small flashes and floating lights as they hovered in my general vicinity. But it wasn't the first time. They were always there, weren't they? "How do I...?" I started to ask, but I already knew the answer. Intention. Vision.

I spun on my heel and headed for The Snug, needing to be alone to do this. I couldn't practise my rusty magick in the face of so many seasoned practitioners. I kicked off my shoes, and paced the room for a while, feeling the cool dusty floor beneath my feet. Eventually, I marked out a circle, creating an imaginary safe space, and set myself inside it. Breathing deeply, I began to clean my mind until the blackness filled me and I was one with myself. When I was ready I allowed the voices and the faces to come.

It was then I recognised, how all of these spirits had been with me all my life. I'd known them as a child, played with some of them, talked to many of them, right until my father disappeared. At that point, with puberty newly upon me, I had rebuffed them. I had denied their existence, their very right to exist, in me or near me. Now I set them free, bade them join me, and assist as they wished and I sensed them swirling around, touching me, the kiss of a spider's web, the light brush of the sparrow's wing, the disturbance in the air as a feather falls to the ground.

With my eyes closed I could see them clearly as they darted here and there, giddy with excitement to be accepted once more. And when I opened my eyes, they were still with me, and I could see their opaque vagueness. Many of them I knew instinctively as my ancestors. I searched among them for my great grandmother, the original Alfhild, but sadly, she was nowhere to be seen. I would seek her out another day.

The ghosts I had managed to summon fluttered around the room like moths, demanding my attention. I bowed to them. "You are welcome here," I said. "And now we have much work to do."

Virginia had been right. Freeing my followers around the inn was a genius solution. They were intent on getting things done, although unfortunately not necessarily in a rational way. They were dragging beds and mattresses down from the attic, while the pixies were still scattering soot left, right and centre. Eventually I was forced to take on the role of a drill sergeant major, ordering things to be done in precisely the right order, barking at pixies, ghosts and witches. Chaos reigned.

Once the pixies had swept the chimneys, I set my ghosts to working at sweeping, dusting and scrubbing. Why had I never thought of this before? In less than two hours the inn, while not gleaming (especially given its dire need for painting and decorating throughout) was cleaner than I had ever known it and the ghosts once more began to drag bedsteads and musty mattresses down from the attic.

I left them to it, after instructing them to air off the mattresses and give them a good beating outside, and found my way into the kitchen where Mortimer was cooking up an amazing roast. The kitchen was a hive of activity, with the highland witches rolling out pastry for a number of sweet and savoury pies, and Bryony making a stuffing for the chicken using breadcrumbs and herbs she'd picked from the garden, and a pâté utilising mushrooms she had foraged in the woods behind the inn.

The woods we intended to fight for.

The plan seemed to be to feast and make merry before sundown. Then we would gather together to create a spell of protection for the inn and the grounds, including Speckled Wood, and cleanse the entire site of negativity and bad energy.

What could possibly go wrong?

I found it quite amazing to witness the amount of food that sixteen people could consume. Our excitement and expectations were high, as was the tension, and our appetites it appeared. Pies, chickens, salads, roast vegetables, pate, bread and crackers – by the time 9 p.m. came around and the sun was dipping towards the horizon, we were all well and truly sated.

I put the ghosts to work on clearing up and washing dishes. It all had to be done 'by hand' as the dish washer in the kitchen had not been operational since I'd moved in. I grimaced as I looked around the kitchen as every pot, pan and mismatched piece of cutlery appeared to have been put to use over the past few hours. There was a mountain of washing up.

Fortunately, while the ghosts had 'no hands' as such, they didn't seem to require them either. As they had demonstrated when they had moved the furniture down from the attic, it all seemed to be a case of mind over matter. I stood at the kitchen door, out of the way, watching as the sink filled itself with water, and copious amounts of washing up liquid created a tower of suds. First glassware, and then crockery flew through the air at break neck speed. The ghosts created something akin to a washing machine rolling action, that involved agitating the soapy water and briskly applying scourers and kitchen cloths. This sent sudsy bubbles floating through the air, rainbows twirling and dancing before popping and leaving an oily residue on the work surfaces. The whole kitchen was getting a workout, that was for sure.

After the initial wash, the plates flew across to the adjoining sink to be dunked in clean water, before ending up on racks, where they paused briefly to drip dry and were then taken up and wiped dry by the apparitions of tea towels, before being flung into cupboards. No breakages – just the loud clang and chink of glasses cosying up to each other, or plates and bowls nestling together in their pre-assigned places.

I found myself awe-struck, a largely hands-off conductor, orchestrating something akin to a scene from Disney's *Fantasia*. Wildly excited by the possibilities my new acceptance of the craft offered, I couldn't wait to get started. I had never seen so much magick in operation as I had done on this day.

Virginia came up behind me, and stood watching with me, evidently enjoying my amusement.

"I should have done this years ago," I said with a giggle. "It would have saved me hours of dull housekeeping."

"You obviously have quite a knack for it," Virginia remarked. "I don't think I've ever seen anyone attract and handle as many spirits at one time as you do."

"What do you mean?"

"I know a few ghost whisperers, and some mediums. Most who work with spirits can summon one or two at a time. Sometimes a few more. It is rare indeed to find someone who can work with this many at once. You have been richly blessed."

I studied the spirits and their various guises. Some wore clothing from the fifteenth and sixteenth centuries, huge collars and ornate patterns visible on their opaque and ornately decorated clothing, others wore powdered wigs or huge Victorian bustles, silk pantaloons or buckled shoes. One was a 1920s flapper, another a world war two soldier, with an arm and a leg missing, but this didn't impede him from racing around the kitchen full of enthusiasm for the task in hand.

"I think they're pleased to have been set loose. They've been cooped up for too long."

Virginia nodded, then gently pulled my arm. "Come," she said. "We are almost ready."

Chapter Twenty-One

Red had busied himself throughout the course of the afternoon by creating a huge pile of wood out the back of the inn. We gathered together, forming a circle around the unlit bonfire, leaving Jed by himself inside – supervising the ghosts if he so wished - with strict instructions not to come outside until we had finished.

We were a quiet group, each thinking our own thoughts, as the sun, burning a bright fiery orange in a pink and peach sky, sunk lower and lower, above the treeline to the west of us. I looked around at the serious faces, wondering who would take charge, hoping against hope that it wouldn't be me. I didn't have an inkling of how we should proceed. Where my magick was concerned, I felt as though I was fumbling in the dark, occasionally striking gold. For something as important as a protection ritual which would encompass both the inn and the whole of my land, I badly needed guidance.

I cleared my throat, about to ask what the plan was, when two figures walked with purpose around from the side of the inn and joined us. I gaped in surprise, Wizard Shadowmender in ceremonial robes and Mr Kephisto in a smart suit and dickie bow, his hair and beard freshly trimmed. Their abrupt appearance was obviously a surprise for the others too, as the sudden exclamations around me indicated.

As he joined the circle, Shadowmender pulled a wand from his robes, uttered the word "*Clauditis*" and casually flicked his wrist. I distinctly heard the locks on the doors around the inn slip into place. "*Caveo et adhamo*," he said and the many windows I had left ajar, in order to allow air to circulate in some of the mustier bedrooms, closed of their own accord, latches dropping into place and bolts being sent home.

Jed had been locked inside. I gazed back, worried about him, home alone. What if there was a fire or a building collapse? I opened my mouth to let Shadowmender know about Jed, but when I turned his way, he looked directly at me and shook his head, ever so slightly.

Shadowmender raised his arms to encompass us all. "Greetings good people, followers of the path, practitioners of the craft, lovers of the earth, disciples of the Goddess. Thank you for answering my call. I chose you to join with me this evening for good reasons, as you will soon realise." Shadowmender indicated me. "We are gathered here this night, primarily to prepare a ritual that will protect Whittle Inn and our sister Alfhild as she goes about her business henceforth."

We all bowed in response to Shadowmender's greeting. Taking this as his cue, Red clapped his hands three times and the wood pile we had surrounded burst into flames with a sudden shower of sparks. I watched these diminutive specks of hot light float away on the slight evening breeze, burning far longer than I would expect, fading to tiny dots of reddy-orange as they reached the edge of the woods, and even then they didn't disappear – simply drifted among the trees to be lost from view. Once they had gone, the blackness there seemed complete and somehow solid. The hair on the back of my neck prickled. I was suddenly certain that something in the woods was watching us.

"We will walk a perimeter that is small and tightly controlled around the inn, chanting and conjuring, envisioning, blessing – whatever. As always, we are free to protect in our own individual ways, and by any means we think are fitting, and when we are certain that no harm will befall the inn, then we will spread out and incorporate the whole of the grounds and the woods beyond."

"Kephisto has kindly taken it upon himself to cast a temporary barrier-holding spell. You will be able to work in and around the area he has mapped out for us, but only until dawn when the barrier will naturally dissipate. It is vitally important that we lock protection in for the whole area – the barrier spell will prevent any overspill into surrounding areas, and help the more adventurous of us remain on-piste, so to speak. Move quickly—dear friends—and with purpose."

Kephisto nodded. "Keep a close eye on where you're heading. You will know the barrier when you see it. Whatever you do, don't break through it. We must keep it intact."

Shadowmender looked gravely around at everyone, and meet their eyes. "Friends, you could have achieved all of this without me," he continued, his voice low, "and without my dear friend Kephisto here. But I asked him to join us as we need his experience. Both he and I suspect that we will all meet some tough resistance as we enter the woods. This is nothing to be sneezed at, I can assure you, and so I issue this warning. Watch your backs. On this very spot in front of us, where the fire burns, a suspected member of The Mori was killed using The Curse of Madb a few weeks ago."

There were audible gasps around the circle.

"Yes indeed. This is a grave situation and potentially highly dangerous. We have no way of knowing who killed him although Kephisto and I have our suspicions as to why. Beware The Mori. I urge you to take good care out there this evening. Arm yourselves," Shadowmender took a deep breath and lifted and dropped his shoulders to relieve some of the tension gathering there, then he smiled, "with your wits if nothing else."

Turning to me, he said, "Alf, if you will insist on being involved, I suggest you stay close to Kephisto or I."

I stared at Shadowmender mutely. Insist on being involved? Did he mean I had a choice? I looked back at the inn where Jed was safely ensconced. I could wait in there with him until all of this was over. But then I looked back at Shadowmender, and as his watery eyes bore into mine, I knew that really there was no choice. I couldn't turn my back on my brothers and sisters of the craft. The time to act to protect the inn was now.

The first part of the ritual pretty much took the shape of the one I had enacted around the inn myself not many day ago. While the majority of the group travelled around the inn chanting and muttering prayers or blessings, invoking various deities, or wafting incense or salt around, others were more static. Bryony sat on the earth with a large silver bowl of water, scrying by the light of the moon. Close by, Shadowmender held his glass orb up to the sky and stared into it, occasionally turning and facing a different way.

For my part, I walked around the perimeter of the inn chanting the same words I had said a few nights previously. The fire in the stables had been meant for the inn, but the inn had been spared thanks to the protection I had woven in place, I was certain of that. Now, as I trailed my hand along the outside of the building, the surface rough beneath my fingers, catching on the sensitive skin around my fingertips, I could feel how Whittle Inn vibrated with a clean and positive energy. With any luck, everything we were doing would ensure Jed remained safe inside.

After a number of turns around the inn, I paused and looked up at the inn. The building shone like a beacon. A colourful aura of red, yellow, orange, blue and green lit up the immediate vicinity. We could do no more, it was time to move into the grounds.

With the building glowing at our backs we began to widen the circle. Wider and wider we walked, in a continuous spiral outward, pacing the same pieces of ground, alternating earth and concrete depending on where we were, stepping among the debris and ash of the stable block. Wider and wider until some time around midnight, I heard the familiar sound of Mr Hoo calling for me, not far from me, through the trees. The undergrowth had become dense.

This was it then. Several of our group had wands out ready, others only their bare hands. I had no comprehension of what I could do, or whether there were any spells I could cast. Instead I stepped into the dark woods, concentrating on cleansing and protection.

Mr Hoo fluttered from branch to branch ahead of me as I walked slowly among the trees, following a natural path. Ahead of me I could vaguely make out Mortimer with his bright yellow shirt. It would be better to take a different route to him, I decided, and so I stepped away from the path, away from him, aware that I had already lost Wizard Shadowmender and Mr Kephisto. I followed a deer trail, watching my step, my eyes gradually adjusting to the poor light, but the darkness was alleviated somewhat by the glowing inn behind me. Then I spotted lights ahead. The words for the ritual died in my throat.

Small orange dots hovered at head height, a few feet away from me. Somewhere else in the world they might have been fireflies, but not here in Devon. They couldn't be. As I moved closer they remained static. I reached out to touch one. It was hot and crumbled to dust in my hand. These were the embers from the fire I had watched as they drifted into the woods. They hung in the air like fairy lights, illuminating a trail for me to follow.

I remained where I was, peering among the trees, the undergrowth and the shadows. From further away I could hear voices, chants and spells and the sounds of people moving carefully through the wood. I wasn't alone by any stretch of the imagination, but now I wished for closer company.

Tentatively I followed the trail of embers, until I

spotted more light ahead. As I moved closer, I could see that it was much larger, hanging in the air, an orb of some description, green with a gold sparkling fleck running through it. Beautiful to look at. At first it was stationary but as I continued to move forwards, it suddenly started spinning extremely quickly and hurtled towards me at speed, I shrieked and ducked as it whizzed past my face close enough to disturb my hair. I spun to see the light hit an oak tree. The massive oak tree, a good eight feet in diameter at the base, rocked in place, and the trunk shimmered green and gold, before gold sparkles exploded into the air and rained down on the ground in front of me. As I bent down to examine the sparkly stuff, Mr Hoo squawked a warning. I felt, rather than saw, something hard volley over the top of my head. Had I been standing upright it would have taken me out. I dropped to my knees and crawled towards the shelter of the oak tree, then peered out from behind the trunk to see what had passed overhead this time.

A red light with gold sparkles hovered some twelve to fourteen feet away from me, pulsing with its own inner energy. The depth of red, the way the gold twisted through it, like a marble, reminded me of the ring that had belonged to the corpse, Edvard Zadzinsky.

Shocked, I threw myself behind the trunk of the oak tree, my breath jerking out of my chest in shallow spasms. Partially immobilised by panic, I clenched my jaw hard. *Get a grip*, I whispered. I needed to warn everyone. I had to take action.

Shouting for help, wishing I'd stayed within shouting distance of Shadowmender or Kephisto after all, I flung myself onto my belly and scuffled through the undergrowth. A scorching beam of red light shot my way, heading directly for me, and I face-planted in the earth, digging my fingers into foliage, willing myself small and insignificant.

The red orbs had to be The Mori. Did that mean the green orbs were friend or foe?

Not far away something exploded, followed by a loud shriek of anger. Hot gold glitter rained down on me when I raised my head to look, and the tree above me pulsed red, green, red and then green before the colours disappeared. When the ground had finished vibrating, I had a quick scout around – I couldn't see any of my friends.

"The Mori are here!" I yelled, hoping my voice would carry and warn everyone else, and then pushed myself to my knees once more and scurried back towards the edge of wood. When nothing else appeared to impede me, I took to my feet and ran, branches catching my hair and yanking me painfully about. Once or twice I lost my footing and crashed to the ground. Any hope I'd had of casting useful spells was lost in my growing panic. I had to get out. I doubled back the way I had come.

Or that's what I thought I was doing.

I found myself face to face with the palest of blue barriers. This was Kephisto's boundary. I had travelled further than I thought. Swivelling to look back, I could see the woods alive with red and green and gold. Explosions lit up the sky like millions of tiny stars, and illuminated the wood. People were running and shouting. The very trees themselves rocked and twisted, branches extended, reaching, whipping backwards and forwards with alarming ferocity, leaves shaking. I heard a crash and then a scream that froze my innards, and without thinking, acting purely on instinct, I stepped away from the chaos. I felt a slight resistance and a pop, and I had breached the barrier, reached the extent of my land and was out of Speckled Wood.

My breath rasped loudly in the silence. Turning slowly, I peered back into my woods and could see nothing extraordinary. No colours. No people. No lights. No blue barrier. Everything appeared as it should, no sense that The Battle for Speckled Wood raged on inside, loud and chaotic and vicious. Less than a mile away people in the village slept easy.

I could walk away. Go back to the inn. Wait for everyone there. Make sure Jed was alright. Then in the morning, all I'd need to do would be to thank everyone for their help, and tell them I'd call them if I ever needed them again. I could live an ordinary, mundane life. Maybe settle down with Jed. Have a few children. Join the WI, become part of the community. Grow old.

Or I could re-join the people in the forest, my people, the ones who had travelled a long way in some cases to help me out. I could fight for my wood and my inn, and banish The Mori from my doorstep, now and forever. Then I could help others to fight The Mori. I could help protect the ancient woods and forests, do something meaningful with my life.

There was no question really. I stepped back towards the action – met the resistance of Kephisto's barrier, which was much stronger this time. I had to really, really want this. I pushed hard, and harder still, stretching at whatever spell he had woven to keep folks out. I was sweating with the strain, urging myself forward and finally I could see the faint blue of the barrier again, and with one more lunge, I plunged back into the fray.

I landed on my knees, instantly on high alert. Uncertain which way to head, I listened. Most of the commotion came from the centre of the woods. I should go that way, towards whatever darkness lurked there. Mr Hoo called to me as I rose.

"I'm back," I whispered to him, brushing the leaves from my knees. "Show me which way to go."

I followed his soft sounds, moving quietly and as quickly as I dared, sticking to the dark paths and shadows.

I thought I was alone, so when someone grabbed my arm I shrieked in fear. Kephisto. His face smudged with dirt and moss. "Are you alright, Alf? I was just checking on the barrier to make sure it was holding."

"I went through it," I garbled. "Did I break it?"

Kephisto looked back towards the inn. "You went all the way through it?" When I nodded, he said, "Then I must check on the inn and recast the spell to keep everything secure. Follow me Alf and keep your head down."

I ducked once more and ran with him, but I had travelled no more than fifty yards or so when something smashed into the tree above my head, and shrieked into my ear so loudly that I was temporarily deafened.

I fell to the ground again, shielding my head, as twigs, small branches, leaves and insects showered down on me. Kephisto had run on without me, oblivious. A red globe of energy, woven with gold, and the size of a cricket ball, shimmered in the air, approximately four feet off the ground. I stared up at it in fear and as I did so I felt something emanating from it, a dark energy, reaching out for me.

"Stay still," a voice from behind me commanded. Not Kephisto.

"It's growing," I said, hearing the tremble in my voice. The orb had grown to the size of a football.

"It's drawing on your negativity. Feeding on your emotion."

The globe pulsed and span in the air, the size of a glitter ball.

I ducked, frightened it would explode and cried out.

"Listen to me," the voice came again, calm and authoritative, and this time I half-thought I recognised it. I turned to see who it was, but could only see shadows behind me. "You have to dampen that fear. Don't feed this creature."

"I don't know how to," I cried, casting a wary eye at the red globe, shimmering in delight above me.

"Yes you do. Kill it with love."

"With love?" I squealed as it whistled and shrieked above me, dancing in place.

From above my head, high up in the tree, I heard Mr Hoo call to me. "Hooo hooo. Hoo hooooo."

Was he safe? My heart melted at the thought of my feathery little friend with his sticky up ears, and that single emotion was enough to halt the globe's relentless spinning and stop it creating such an awful noise. It hung in the air, the colour diminishing. I conjured up Mr Hoo's face in my mind's eye and smiled, imagined smoothing his feathers, balancing him on one hand, feeling his weightlessness. As I did so, the gold shimmer disappeared from the globe as it began to shrink. I imagined lifting my arm, and Mr Hoo leaping away, flying though Speckled Wood, hunting in the night, free and happy. The globe shrank ever smaller until eventually it collapsed in on itself and disappeared with a pop.

Relieved, I scrambled to my feet once more. I turned to thank my saviour, but he had disappeared. No time to waste, and crouching low to avoid incoming missiles I ran towards the action, now relatively unafraid. I had the capacity to defeat these things, after all. I passed a number of our group, magnificent in their fearlessness and tenacity, engaging more of the red globes, each dealing with them in their own way. I spared a moment to contemplate that this Battle for Speckled Wood would surely go down in the magickal history books, as I reached the clearing in the centre of the forest where the circle of benches had been arranged. Pausing to take stock of what to do next, and half hoping I would draw out another of the enemy, I heard someone yelling, "We've got them on the run!"

Thrilled, I clapped my hands, and in the same instant heard Mr Hoo calling to me urgently. I turned to look for him and was knocked off my feet by a pulse of bright corrupt energy, landing with a painful thump on my right hip and elbow, and smacking my head on the ground. After lying dazed for a few seconds, I struggled to sit up.

A large red globe apparated in front of me. This one was different to the others, larger, a deeper red. The weave of gold through the centre was beaded and ornate. I tried to keep my fear in check, watching as it started to grow, swelling to twice and then three times its original size until it was the size of a horse, hovering mere inches above the ground.

I rubbed the side of my head and heard others joining me. Wizard Shadowmender, wand drawn, Kephisto, his hands stretched out, Mortimer and Virginia, Bryony bleeding from a gash on her forehead, Finbarr with a potential black eye ... and behind us all, the green globes created a circle around the clearing, forming a barrier of sorts. Our adversary could not escape.

Energy flew from the red ball in spiky shots of lightning, downing several of the green balls, shrieks split the air around us, and I could see that a number of the green globes, and our witches were ready to cut it down. But Shadowmender dropped his wand and held his left hand up.

"No more," he said, his voice quiet but firm, and the tension that had been ramped up, eased a little.

Mr Kephisto helped me to my feet, and I stood in between him and Wizard Shadowmender as the latter addressed the red globe.

"We have banished The Mori from this wood tonight, and you – their leader - are the last, and the angriest. This is no place for you. You may leave of your own free will or you will be exiled. Fight us and we will destroy you. The choice is yours."

The globe in the centre of the clearing spun dizzyingly quickly, gold sparks flying through the air and illuminating the surroundings. I noticed two figures lying prone on the floor, at the edge of the clearing, clad all in dark green. These were the green globes, now transitioned from energy to bodies.

"Wait," I said. "Who are you? Show yourself."

I caught the glance between Shadowmender and Kephisto. "I want to see. I want to know who wishes ill on the inn and the forest."

Kephisto nodded and Shadowmender lifted his wand. "Show yourself," he commanded and the globe stopped spinning, and shrank rapidly, settling on the ground, revealing a figure clad in a dull red cloak, hiding his features from view. When he moved, a bright ruby ring shone on his hand. And then he stood, tall and fierce, dark-haired and handsome in his own unique way, and entirely unapologetic.

"Jed!" I cried in surprise, and my heart shattered.

Jed stood tall, his demeanour difficult to read. He was beaten and he knew it. He glared at us all one by one, turning to take everyone in, leaving no-one out, his look one of utter disdain and hatred. I watched him do this and I willed myself to be strong. I would not let him fell me with his loathing. He left me till last. The Alf of six or eight weeks ago would have withered and died. But not me. Not today.

I stepped forward to meet him and stretched my hands out to his face.

"Alf," Shadowmender said behind me, but I shrugged him off.

I didn't touch Jed, just held my hands an inch from each side of his face as though I would reach to caress him, hold him close and kiss him, as I had done dozens of times over the last few weeks. I'd been blinded by my feelings. In this moment, I could have said, "I thought you loved me," because I thought he had, but that wasn't important any more.

Instead, in a calm quiet voice, I told him the things that were important. "I love you. Thank you for helping me find myself. Thank you for helping me to fall in love with the inn. Thank you for helping me to see my future and my place in it."

Later I would think it was my imagination, because no-one else noticed a change in expression, but I thought I caught something in his eyes. Regret? Perhaps.

"You can't hurt us now. Not me, nor my friends, not the inn or Speckled Wood," I said. "I banish you from this place. Never visit my hearth or darken my door again. You are not welcome in these woods, and neither are your kind." I stepped away from him, then slowly turned to take in my friends, indicating that everyone else should join me in Jed's expulsion.

"We set you free, to live your live in peace and harmony elsewhere." I lifted my hand, palm up. "Goodbye Jed," I said and pushed at the air between us. The very earth seemed to move beneath my feet, and such a force of magick erupted around me as my friends joined me, that the world crackled as though held in the grip of a furious fire. And then Jed, and all of The Mori, were gone.

CHAPTER TWENTY-TWO

My shoulders slumped as I regarded the empty space he'd once inhabited. With Jed in my life I had certainly felt less alone. I heard mumbling around me and sensed movement as my friends shuffled about, exclaiming at aches and pains. I turned about. The first fingers of dawn were poking at the sky, and one by one the stars were flickering out.

Kephisto and Shadowmender stood together, each observing me with compassion.

"You knew, didn't you?" I asked and Shadowmender nodded.

"I'm afraid so. When you came to see me, I knew some of what was going on because Millicent had been keeping me informed, and you filled in the blanks. When I asked you to hold the orb, I'd already requested that it show you who was leading the campaign of destruction against you and the inn.

The first person you saw would be the perpetrator of ills against you."

"I saw Jed," I said dully. "I thought that was because I'd left him at the inn to look after things, so the orb was merely showing me what was."

"His magick was effective because you had freely invited him to be part of your life, and because you trusted him."

"Millicent recommended him to me," I pointed out.

"Yes, she's been working underground for us here in Whittlecombe for years. Her role in this was twofold. She has always kept an eye on happenings at the inn, in your family's absence in any case. But most importantly, she has long suspected Jed's father of being a member of The Mori, so we decided to bring you and Jed together and see what that would teach us. Millicent has proved her mettle time and time again. I am sorry that you had feelings for Jed. That was an unplanned consequence."

My head was spinning. People I had trusted were not who I thought they were, and some of those I suspected were entirely trustworthy. How had I missed all the signs? "He knew all my weaknesses. I confessed everything to him. It could have been so easy for him to destroy both me and the inn."

"You're a good person, Alf," Mr Kephisto said quietly. "You will move on from this."

"I sent you to Mr Kephisto after you had visited me, so he'd confirm my suspicions," Shadowmender continued. "We were worried about you."

"I needed you to stay the night, to keep an eye on you," Kephisto added. The two wizards appeared to be perfectly in tune with each other's thinking.

"You put something to my tea?" I realised. "Yes, enough to knock me out there and then, but not enough to stop me from worrying."

"I gave you a mild sedative."

I shook my head. "I guess it was all for the best."

"I'm sorry. I went through your phone while you were asleep. I wanted to see photos of Jed. I recognised him, mostly because of how similar he looks to his father at that age. His father is a very big noise among The Mori. He defected from the Circle of Querkus many years ago. It seems Jed is intent on following in his dad's dark footsteps."

"So Jed is the one that's been in league with Talbot-Lloyd and Pimm?" I asked and Shadowmender nodded.

"The good news is that we can sort all that out now. Take care of things so that you won't be bothered by the local officials."

"What about Penelope Quigwell?" I asked, and saw Mr Kephisto mask a smirk.

"Don't worry about Penelope," Shadowmender responded smiling. "She's ... an oddball certainly, and can be abrupt and a little haughty, but believe me, she's wonderful at what she does. She's been working with me for decades. You'll find that the inn's accounting and all your legal affairs are perfectly in order."

"Alright," I said, weary now. I suppose at some stage I would have to start trusting again, but it might take some time. I shook my head, thinking bleakly of Jed. "He had me fooled. I thought I could trust him. I thought he was ... my friend."

A gentle hooing noise from beside me drew my attention. Mr Hoo had fluttered down to perch on the bench beside me. I smiled at him. "Thank you. You *are* my little friend," I said. "Sterling work little fella." I smoothed his feathers. "You don't have much of the night left, you should get to your hunting. I'll see you this evening."

"Hoo-ooo," the owl responded, and took flight in an explosion of feathers and dust.

I watched him go, fondly. With Mr Hoo in situ, I wouldn't be totally alone at the inn tonight after all.

Wizard Shadowmender threw his arm across my

shoulders. “Come this way, Alf. There’s something else you need to know. And someone you should meet,” he said, and led me out of the clearing to where two of the green globes were hanging about. The rest had dissipated into the woods. I watched this pair as they span, ever quicker, and then, with a blinding flash shattered in a fantastic shimmering explosion. In their place stood a man in his fifties, and a woman, far older.

“Alf,” said the man, and there was a warmth in his voice that melted my soul. The voice I’d heard in the woods when I’d encountered the red globe. A voice from my past.

“Dad?” I asked in disbelief, stepping forwards to stare into the man’s face. I gazed up at him, at his clear wise eyes. The hair was longer, greyer, the appearance more lived in, his face more jowly, but it was indeed my father. “Dad?” I asked again, my voice breaking. “Where have you been? Why did you go away?” And then with my arms wrapped around him, I sobbed my broken heart out.

“I had to follow my calling,” Dad told me, as we made ourselves comfortable back at the inn. He had introduced me to the older woman, known only as Anima, and she sat with us, in a quiet corner of the reception area, as Wizard Shadowmender and Mr Kephisto huddled at the bar discussing the night's events and their next move.

We had—all of us—trekked back through the woods. I was relieved to find the inn safe and sound. Some members of the group headed straight for bed, others wanted baths. I disturbed the ghosts as I entered, mentally shook them awake. "How about breakfast?" I asked them. "And find more seats. And towels." They leapt to the challenge, flying around the inn, lighting the big fire in the grate and sending chairs down from the attic. Baths were run, towels located. The kitchen rang to the noise of crockery and pots and pans flying around the room, bacon sizzled and eggs were beaten.

At one stage I thought I heard a cow mooing.

I don't own a cow.

I didn't go and check.

Instead I sat next to my Dad and held onto both his hand and his every word. He described how his calling had been to become a member of the Circle of Querkus, and how ever since he'd been a boy, playing in Speckled Wood with Millicent, he had wanted to nourish the environment and cherish our green spaces.

"Your mother understood," he told me. "She wanted me to follow my heart. I joined the Circle of Querkus to help them guard the forests ... and fight The Mori. I have been the guardian of Speckled Wood ever since, watching over the inn and its inhabitants."

"You killed Edvard Zadzinsky?" I asked.

"Yes. He came upon me in Speckled Wood one day and took me by surprise. I hadn't realised The Mori had made a move into Whittlecombe."

"You used The Curse of Madb?"

"I did. He had already attacked me. If I hadn't killed him first, he would have killed me."

I remembered stumbling across the burn mark in the clearing on my first walk in the wood. "And then you moved him."

"I knew from Shadowmender that you were on your way to the inn. I wanted to find a way to warn you of the danger. Perhaps even warn you off entirely."

"You didn't see that I would fall in love with this old place," I replied, looking around fondly at the exposed beams and original features. The inn was buzzing with the goings-on. Ghosts and witches and pixies and warlocks and who knows what else. "Why couldn't we all have lived here, back in the day? Couldn't mother and I have come here and stayed with you?" I asked.

"We both felt that you would be safer away from the inn and the forests here. I couldn't abide the thought that you might be caught up in The Mori's evil. I wanted you to be protected until you came of age, and I would pass the inn on to you. What I hadn't accounted for was how stubborn you are. I didn't for one moment think you would forsake the craft and fall out with your mother."

"Oh dear," I said, cringing as I remembered the arguments, and regretting the years of angst between myself and my mother. "I did her a huge disservice. She was trying to protect me, and I thought she was interfering in my life."

"We seem to have gone about this all the wrong way," my father said mournfully.

"Couldn't you have been a member of the Circle of Querkus and lived here at the inn?" I asked but he shook his head.

"No," he replied simply, "because I'm no longer alive."

My heart stopped. "What do you mean?" I leant

forward in my seat, to prod him. He felt solid enough.

"I'm not a spirit like these," he gestured at the various ghosts in the room supervising flying teapots and mugs, and knives and forks that flew through the air like arrows intended for hungry victims. "But I no longer exist on the mortal plane." He gestured at Anima, who had been quietly listening to our conversation. "The Circle of Querkus live half in the spirit world, and half on the earth. We inhabit the globes of energy that you saw in the woods. They are shells, our minds reside within. They allow us to travel superfast and at will. They are an effective weapon against The Mori, although of course The Mori use their own similar device."

"So you're still dead," I said sadly, and my father reached for my hand.

"I am," he said, "but you are not alone anymore, not least because you have stepped into your own powers. You'll find that Penelope has all of the accounts up to date, and there is money enough for you to finish renovating the inn, and spread a little love among the properties in the village. You will make this inn something wonderful with the help of the spirits you call to your side. And remember this: I too am part spirit and you can therefore call me to you at will. Whenever you need me, come to the clearing in Speckled Wood and summon me. I'll be here in a flash."

"And in the meantime you're still the guardian of Speckled Wood?" I asked.

He nodded. "And you're the saviour of Whittle Inn."

EPILOGUE

A few days later I found myself in a clearing in a different forest, where several months before I had witnessed Wizard Shadowmender hold the funeral ceremony for my mother. So much had changed since then, most of all within myself. I wanted to make reparations, and to that end, I built a small fire and once it had taken hold, added damp moss to the flames to make it smoke.

I stood in front of the fire, blinking as the smoke blew into my eyes, then dashing away my tears. I commanded an image of my mother to me. Her face appeared as plain as day and I smiled to see her.

I unfolded a letter I had written to her, and read it out.

Dear Yasmine

"I'm sorry," it said. *"It was wrong of you and Dad to*

keep the truth from me, but I behaved badly too. I can see now that you were trying to prepare me for the life you imagined I would lead, and it must have been a disappointment to you when I lost my taste for magick.

I want to let you know that I have found my way back. And that I am learning more every day. I'm going to keep right on, practicing my skills, and summoning my spirits, and I hope one day that I will be half the witch you were, and half the warlock my father was. I intend to keep a righteous route, to err on the side of good, and stay away from the dark path.

But you should also know that when I turned my face away from the craft, it was not time wasted. Quite the reverse. My life among mortals taught me all about hospitality, and running a business, particularly the inn.

So Mother, we should take comfort in the fact that in the end, we were both right for different reasons.

I'm opening my inn, but not in direct competition with The Hay Loft in Whittlecombe. I remember that a friend in the village, Rhona, told me I should consider my target market, and given the enormous success I've had over the past few days, entertaining witches, wizards, druids, warlocks and seers – among

others – I think I know exactly who my clientele will be in the future.
All things resolve themselves in the end, and I am only sorry that I wasn't able to tell you that I love you before you departed this plane. Perhaps one day, when we are both ready, I will call your spirit and we can sit and yarn about the old days.
Your ever loving daughter
Alfhild

I took a deep breath and fed the letter to the fire, watching as it stubbornly held onto its physical form, until at last the flames caught it and gobbled it up greedily. I could see the ghost of the shape of the paper for long seconds, until at last it crumbled to ash and fell into the heart of the fire.

Remaining where I was for a few more minutes, I tilted my head back to watch the grey smoke drift up into the milky sky above. Was it my imagination or could I see the outline of my lopsided hostelry taking shape up there?

Smiling, I turned for home. The wonkiest witch heading back to her wonky inn.

The end

NEED MORE WONKY?

The series continues in Wonky Inn Book 2 – *The Ghosts of Wonky Inn*

Alf has tried to banish her demons.
And her ghosts. But memories of Jed linger and keep her awake.

Every night it's the same. When she does eventually drift off, she's woken almost immediately by a sobbing spirit.

He's lost. And worse than that, someone is trying to kill him. Who is this sad specimen of a spirit? And where does he belong?

And how do you kill someone ... who is already dead?

Find out what Alf gets up to next.

Preorder *The Ghosts of Wonky Inn* now! And don't miss the Wonky Inn Christmas Special.
The Witch who killed Christmas

Both available from Amazon

ACKNOWLEDGEMENTS

What started out as an experiment, rapidly became all consuming. I wasn't sure it was possible for me to write clean and cozy, because I am so used to living on the dark side with my other work. However, as Alf's story began to come alive, I totally fell in love with her and the other wonderful assortment of characters contained in this novel.
So much so, that I knew there needed to be more. I hope that's good news!

I have a growing street team: Jeannie Wycherley's Fiendish Author Street Team, who are so engaged and supportive that it is a little like having a cheerleading squad. Given that I'm British, and rather laid back (okay – introverted), this is odd, but wonderful. I can certainly get used to it!

High fives are therefore due to Debbie Rodriguez, Rosemary Kenney, Heaven Riendeau, Bax Al,

Morag Fowler and Sandra Tickner-Hobson, among others.

I couldn't do any of this without my husband, John Wycherley, and this year he has really pushed me to go for it. Similarly, my author bestie, Julie Archer, continues to be in my corner - and mailbox - whenever I need a kick up the backside. Big loves! Go and check out Julie's work – what are you waiting for?

Special thanks are due to two new-to-me people who take what I'm doing very seriously. Firstly, JC Clarke of The Graphics Shed for her phenomenal covers. Not just *The Wonkiest Witch* but the next four in the series too! I am blown away. Wait till you see them.

And secondly to Anna Bloom, who is not just a wonderful editor - constructive, strict but funny, kind and compassionate too - she's a pretty phenomenal mentor as well. The Wonky Inn series will be amazing, because she believes in it, and me, and that makes a huge difference.

Finally, thanks to you, the reader. I love bringing you

stories, reading your reviews, and receiving your feedback.

You complete my circle.
Much love ♥
Jeannie Wycherley
Devon, UK
31st October 2018

Coming Soon

Coming Winter 2018/2019

The Municipality of Lost Souls by Jeannie Wycherley

Described as a cross between Daphne Du Maurier's *Jamaica Inn*, and TV's *The Walking Dead*, but with ghosts instead of zombies, *The Municipality of Lost Souls* tells the story of Amelia Fliss and her cousin Agatha Wick.

In the otherwise quiet municipality of Durscombe, the inhabitants of the small seaside town harbour a deadly secret.

Amelia Fliss, wife of a wealthy merchant, is the lone voice who speaks out against the deadly practice of the wrecking and plundering of ships on the rocks in Lyme bay, but no-one appears to be listening to her.

As evil and malcontent spread like cholera throughout the community, and the locals point fingers and vow to take vengeance against outsiders, the dead take it upon themselves to end a barbaric tradition the living seem to lack the will to stop.

Set in Devon in the UK during the 1860s, *The Municipality of Lost Souls* is a Victorian Gothic ghost story, with characters who will leave their mark on you forever.

If you enjoyed *Beyond the Veil*, you really don't want to miss this novel.

Sign up for my newsletter or join my Facebook group today.

FIND THE AUTHOR

Please consider leaving a review?
If you have enjoyed reading *The Wonkiest Witch: Wonky Inn Book 1*, please consider leaving me a review.

Reviews help to spread the word about my writing, which takes me a step closer to my dream of writing full time.

If you are kind enough to leave a review, please also consider joining my Author Street Team on Facebook – **Jeannie Wycherley's Fiendish Street Team.** Do let me know you left a review when you apply because it's a closed group.

You can find my fiendish team at
www.facebook.com/groups/JeannieWycherleysFiends

You'll have the chance to Beta read and get your hands on advanced review eBook copies from time to time. I also appreciate your input when I need some help with covers, blurbs etc.

Follow Jeannie Wycherley

Find out more at on the website
www.jeanniewycherley.co.uk

You can tweet Jeannie
twitter.com/Thecushionlady

Or visit her on Facebook for her fiction
www.facebook.com/jeanniewycherley

Sign up for Jeannie's newsletter
http://eepurl.com/cN3Q6L

ALSO BY

Beyond the Veil

Crone

A Concerto for the Dead and Dying

Deadly Encounters: A collection of short stories

Keepers of the Flame: A love story

Non Fiction

Losing my best Friend

Thoughtful support for those affected by dog bereavement or pet loss

CPSIA information can be obtained
at www.ICGtesting.com
Printed in the USA
LVHW041529220723
753177LV00004B/66